About the Author

The author grew up in Oadby, Leicestershire. During her teens, she moved to Nottingham with her parents, where she met her future husband, David. After her career in retail management, she and her husband spent their early retirement in Pembrokeshire. She now lives in Moraira, Spain with David.

The Verdant Haven

Emily Parr

The Verdant Haven

Olympia Publishers
London

www.olympiapublishers.com
OLYMPIA PAPERBACK EDITION

Copyright ©Emily Parr 2019

The right of Emily Parr to be identified as author of
this work has been asserted in accordance with sections 77 and 78 of the Copyright, Designs and Patents Act 1988.

All Rights Reserved

No reproduction, copy or transmission of this publication
may be made without written permission.
No paragraph of this publication may be reproduced,
copied or transmitted save with the written permission of the publisher, or in accordance with the provisions
of the Copyright Act 1956 (as amended).

Any person who commits any unauthorised act in relation to
this publication may be liable to criminal
prosecution and civil claims for damage.

A CIP catalogue record for this title is
available from the British Library.

ISBN: 978-1-78830-221-0

This is a work of fiction.
Names, characters, places and incidents originate from the writer's imagination. Any resemblance to actual persons, living or dead, is purely coincidental.

First Published in 2019

Olympia Publishers
60 Cannon Street
London
EC4N 6NP

Printed in Great Britain

Dedication

For my late cousin, Ann.

Acknowledgments

My thanks go to cousin Chris, for reading the drafts, providing the cover photograph, and for being my critic. And to my husband, David, for his constant love and support.

Chapter One
January 1939

The meeting, held by the Reverend Alex Pritchard in Manddiogel's village hall, in response to the BBC's Foster Home appeal for children at risk in Central Europe, drew to a close. He addressed those in attendance. "If anyone feels able to offer a home to a child, there are several things you should consider: there will be no financial help, and we don't know how long it will be for. The child will be Jewish and unlikely to speak any English, and of course there will be cultural and domestic differences to overcome." Stan and Nancy Morgan, of Gorse Wen Farm, were interested; they told the minister it was likely that he would be able to put their names forward.

Later that evening, Stan told his teenage sons Glynn and Tom about the plight of certain people in Europe, and the urgency of getting vulnerable children to safety; he mentioned the possibility of a child coming to live with them for a while, and asked what they thought about it. "I don't mind, do you Glynn?" asked Tom, looking at his elder brother.

"No, it's all right with me," replied Glynn. "Will it be a boy or a girl?"

"We don't know at this stage—we don't mind, although I'd quite like a young child," said his mother. "I don't think your dad minds either, do you, Dad?"

"Not really; an older boy would be useful to have on the farm, but if war breaks out, he'll probably get called up, eventually."

"Is there going to be another war?" asked Tom.

"I don't know, son; I daresay they'll try to avoid it. No one will want to go through all that again in a hurry."

Nancy needed her sons to understand that this was not going to be an easy undertaking; she told them that the child would be frightened, and that almost everything they said or did would be unfamiliar. "Our food, way of life, the school and the chapel will seem very strange at first; we must consider every aspect and try to foresee how it will impact on the child." The boys understood, and agreed this was something they wanted to do; Stan informed the minister, and their details were sent to the British government. Before long there was confirmation that a girl aged six was on her way.

***

The monstrous locomotive belched the remains of its smoke, and steam from the boiler escaped with a huge sigh; every carriage was packed with children fleeing the terrors of the Third Reich in Germany and its surrounding neighbours. Many had been orphaned as a result of the Holocaust gaining momentum, or their parents having been imprisoned in concentration camps. Some had been sent to Britain by their parents when persecution and confiscation made it essential to leave and find sanctuary elsewhere. There were few very young ones on this trip; most were aged between eight and thirteen.

There was only one escort, this time: George Richardson, from Middlesbrough. He had been a member of the group of

Quakers and Jews who had persuaded Prime Minister Neville Chamberlain to speed up the evacuation process for the most vulnerable children in Germany, Czechoslovakia, Austria, and Poland. He was now a representative of the British Government, working in Germany, helping oversee the organisation and transportation of evacuees to Britain. He didn't often travel with the children to the coastal port in Holland, only if there was a need to spot-check the embarkation procedure, or if there was no other escort available.

After seeing all the children safely on board, the boat set sail for Harwich, George waited while the locomotive was turned round on the turntable and the carriages connected, in readiness for its return journey to Dortmund.

The channel crossing was rough. Most of the children had been sick, and all of them were frightened and cold; the escorts on the boat tried to keep them occupied with games and donated toys, but it was difficult, because of the language barrier. They felt thoroughly washed out and sick themselves, so it was decided to let the children form groups and play together naturally.

After the boat docked, the children were taken to a holding building near the wharf; German and Polish speakers ushered the children toward reception desks manned with serious-looking personnel. Each child was taken to a desk, where their personal details were given to the official.

After registration, they were put into appropriate groups and taken to the yard, where several coaches and cars were waiting. Those allocated a home in the east of England or the Midlands boarded the vehicles and left. About a hundred were going to homes farther afield, in places such as Wales, Scotland, and Cornwall. They travelled by train to Liverpool Street Station in London, where escorts waited to supervise their onward journeys. Some children had no home yet; they were going to stay at the Dovercourt Holiday Camp nearby until one was found.

Eva Aarons, a small Jewish girl aged six, was on the train bound for Liverpool Street Station; on arrival, she and a few other children were taken by bus to Paddington Station, where the Cardiff train was waiting.

She stood nervously by her suitcase on the platform in Cardiff Station, and watched the lady who had travelled with her speaking to a man and woman. She turned to Eva, and, in simple German, said, "Eva, this is Mr. and Mrs. Morgan; they are going to take you to their home, and they will look after you until Mama and Papa find a safe place for you to live."

Addressing Stan and Nancy, she said, "Thank you for your generosity, Mr. and Mrs. Morgan, it is appreciated. Goodbye." Turning to Eva she gently said, "Goodbye, Eva."

"Come, Eva," said Nancy, holding out her hand to the child. While sucking her left thumb, Eva gingerly put her right hand into Nancy's. Stan picked up the small suitcase; the three of them left the station building and went to the car park, where Rusty, one of the farm dogs, was waiting in the old Bedford pick-up. As they approached he sprang to the window, and when the door opened he jumped out and greeted them with great excitement. Not being used to dogs, Eva hid behind Nancy in fear.

"Down, Rusty!" At Stan's command the dog calmed and watched his master expectantly; his feathery tail was brushing the tarmac while he waited for his accustomed pat. Stan took Eva's hand and showed her how to gently stroke the top of Rusty's head. Nancy said, "I'll sit in the back between Rusty and Eva; she'll soon get used to him."

Up and along the road to the Valleys, past steep hills cheerfully coloured with gorse and heather, the truck and its occupants made their way home; the broody leaden sky, threatening a deluge, could never spoil the beauty of this landscape, although farther into the valley large areas had been spoilt by the colliery. The slag heap and the mine's blackened buildings, the dark terraces of miners' dwellings, and the coal-dust, covering everything in grime, created a gloomy scene.

After passing through the village, Stan turned the Bedford into the muddy, pot-holed track that led to Gorse Wen Farm. It had a good aspect on a hillside, and the well-drained land was rich pasture; ancient water courses ran along its boundaries and into the small river at its lowest level.

Stan and Nancy were sheep farmers. They also kept a few goats, an assortment of fowl, and grew vegetables that could withstand the harsh climate. They managed to live quite well during hard times, because produce from the farm was sold in the village, along with Nancy's pies, cakes, and cheeses; some women preferred to buy directly from Nancy's kitchen, knowing that there would be a warm welcome and a chat. At certain times of the year, Stan carried out maintenance on other premises for payment in kind. He was passing his skills on to his sons, because good quality workmanship was in demand, especially hedge-laying and dry stone walling. Not everyone could do it, or was fit enough to do so.

Stan stopped the truck at the back door to let the occupants out; he then drove to the barn and parked it there. Glynn and Tom were in the woods clearing brambles and fallen branches; before she had left to collect Eva that morning, Nancy had asked them to stay out of the house while she settled Eva, because she didn't want her overwhelmed, especially after such an arduous journey. She took the silent child into the kitchen, where she removed her coat and washed her hands and face.

It was time to eat the cawl that had slowly cooked while they had been away. Nancy noticed that the dining chair was too low for Eva, so she fetched a couple of cushions for her. Stan came in, winked at Eva and sat on his chair at the head of the table, while Nancy ladled the cawl on to three plates. Eva picked at hers at first, but when she realised it tasted nice, she ate hungrily, and had a second helping.

"What's for afters, Nan?" Stan asked hopefully.

"Jam roly poly, although I'd like to get Eva bathed and into bed first. Why not spend half an hour with the boys? If you like, you can have some more dinner when they have theirs, and we can eat our puddings together."

Stan noticed Meg, his border collie, lying by the range, regarding him with expectation in her old loving eyes. "Come on then," he said, and off they went to find the boys.

Nancy loved Meg. Stan had bought her nine years previously, when she was a puppy, from an auction in Maerdy. He worked her alongside his experienced sheep-dog Kip, knowing that one day she would take his place. When old Kip died, she became Stan's right hand. In all weathers, they brought the sheep down to the lower pasture for lambing or shearing, and back on to the hills for the summer months. She was a tired old dog now, and spent most of her time dozing by the range in Nancy's kitchen, yet was always ready to accompany her master in the fields, if he wasn't in a hurry. The farm's working dogs were Meg's offspring; puppies from her previous litters were working on farms in Powys and Glamorgan, and some even further afield.

Rusty was her companion. Tom had brought him home after finding him frightened and abandoned in a ditch a few years previously. "All right," Stan had said to the two imploring faces looking up at him, "you may keep him, but he's your dog, so don't expect Mam to look after him." With that agreed, the two boys kept the dog, and the three grew up together. In the early days Rusty slept in Tom's room at night, and waited for him to return from school; at weekends, he explored the hills with the boys and their friends. But Glynn and Tom were grown now, and busy on the farm; if they were working with the collies, he stayed in the kitchen with Meg, and watched Nancy's every move when she made those tasty lamb cawls and pies.

Meg can help me with Eva; she'll be a good companion, she thought, as she poured warm water into the small tin bath she had used when Glynn and Tom were small. She helped Eva climb off the chair when her dinner was finished, and led her to the bath in front of the range. She carefully removed her clothing and helped her to step into the bath; she put a toy in the water for her to play with, but there was no reaction.

With hair washed and rinsed with a splash of vinegar in the final jugful, and a good flannelling with carbolic soap, Eva was spotless. Nancy helped her out of the bath and dried her in front of the warm range; she noticed a few red patches on her skin, so she rubbed in some zinc and castor oil. The nightie which Mrs. Evans's daughter, Jeannie, had outgrown was slipped on, and Eva was ready for bed.

Still she hadn't uttered a word, but what could she say? She knew no English words; all she had done so far was to suck her thumb and gaze with blank eyes.

Nancy sat in Stan's old leather chair by the fire, and lifted Eva on to her ample knee; within moments, the child was fast asleep with her thumb in her mouth. She relished having this elfin girl in her arms; she smelled her clean brown curls and made a vow to protect this little angel, and keep her safe until her mother was able to take her home.

This is how Stan and their two sons found them almost an hour later when they returned from the woods, "Make a brew, Tom, there's a good lad," said Stan, getting organised. "Glynn, get rid of that water and swill the bath in the yard, please, while I help Mam get Eva into bed; then we'll have our dinner."

"I'll take this little one," he said, lifting the sleeping girl off his wife's knee. Nancy went upstairs to Eva's room, followed by Stan, carrying Eva in his powerful arms; he laid her in the bed and tucked her in. "Isn't she lovely?" said Nancy, sadly, wishing that their baby daughter had lived.

"Aye, she is that, Nan," agreed Stan ruefully.

The kitchen was chaotic, with a mixed aroma of pudding steaming over a pan of boiling water, cawl, carbolic soap, vinegar, and dogs. Meg and Rusty were getting under everyone's feet, knowing that something was going on; the hungry boys were waiting for their dinner; and the exhausted girl's suitcase and clothes were still on the floor where Nancy had left them.

"Glynn, are you going out tonight?" asked Nancy of her eldest son.

"Yes, just to the club," he replied, wondering if he would be able to use the sink before it was needed for the washing up.

"As soon as you've had your dinner, use the sink, but be quick about it; I've a lot to do tonight. What about you, Tom?" she asked, turning to her youngest.

"I want to work on my glider; may I use the table?" He was making a model out of balsa wood; Stan and Nancy had bought him the kit last Christmas.

"Yes, I won't need it," she replied. "Do you want another plate of cawl?" she asked Stan, passing Glynn and Tom theirs.

When her three men were eating their dinners, she made a start on the custard.

All four, seated at the table eating their puddings, talked about the day's events; the boys were eager to hear about the trip to Cardiff Station and the journey through the valley. They rarely left their village; if they did, it was never as far as Cardiff.

A couple of hours later, Glynn was at the Miners' Welfare with his friends and, as Nancy had suspected, Ginny Price from the bakery. Tom was shaving a lump of balsa, which was going to be the fuselage, and Stan was chuffing on his pipe by the fire, with Meg and Rusty at his feet. Nancy cleared away the clean pots and pans and draped the damp tea towel over the warm rail on the range door; she picked up Eva's travelling clothes and took them to the sink. She opened the suitcase. Inside, she found a few items of clothing, a cloth rabbit, a hair brush and comb, and a photograph of a young family. She thought the clothes could do with freshening; they were clean, but she sensed the sooty smell of the train and dampness from the journey, so she put them by the sink with the other things. She took the case up to Eva's room and propped the photograph against the flower vase, on top of the chest of drawers, putting the brush and comb by its side. The case and shoes went into the closet, and the rabbit was placed in the bed next to Eva. Afterwards, she went into the front bedroom where she and Stan slept; she sat on the bed for a few moments, and wept.

"All right, Nan?" asked Stan when she returned to the kitchen.

"Yes, she's sleeping like a top, I'm just going to rinse her clothes through to get the journey out of them."

"Can't it wait until tomorrow?"

"If I do it now, they'll dry on the rack during the night. Miss Hughes from the school is coming tomorrow; she's going to go through the English learning pack with me and she'll probably want to get Eva started with some words to practice over the weekend. I don't want any washing around while she's here." It took a few minutes to freshen Eva's clothes; Nancy hung them to dry on the ceiling rack near the range and sat down with her knitting. It was a pleasant change to use pretty yellow wool after years of knitting with dark earthy colours. The first raglan sleeve of Eva's new jumper was almost finished; if she made the other one tomorrow, she would be able to wear it to chapel on Sunday under the pinafore which Mary Jenkins had made from a spare piece of corduroy.

As soon as Eva woke the following morning, she knew something had happened during the night. It had happened before; Mama said it started after those bad men destroyed their shop. She started to cry and the lady came upstairs and into the room; she pulled back the bedclothes and said something Eva didn't understand. She recognised the tone though, it sounded a bit like when Mama said, "It's all right, there's no need to cry, get up." Eva got out of bed, the lady removed her nightie and the damp sheet and took her downstairs; she was washed and dressed, and given a beaker of sweet milky tea.

She was playing with the dogs when a visitor came to the house with a bag of books and papers; the visitor sat with the lady at the kitchen table and discussed the contents of the bag with her. After a while, the ladies had her join them at the table.

The visitor took one of the books from the pile; on the first page there was a picture of a red apple with 'Aa', and the word 'Apple' next to it. The following page displayed a blue ball with 'Bb', and the word 'Ball'; each one had a different picture and word. This was familiar to Eva; she had seen a book like this at kindergarten. Most of the pictures were similar, just in a different sequence. The apple page was the same, and so was the ball, but in the kindergarten book the picture of the cat didn't follow that of the ball, and it said 'Kk, Katze', not 'Cc, Cat' as this one did. The visitor continued to turn the pages, pausing at each one to say, and to have Eva repeat, the word printed next to the objects in the pictures.

Once the concept of the alphabet book appeared to be understood, the visitor wrote the words MISS HUGHES in a note book and showed it to Eva, she spoke the words while putting her hand on her own chest. She had Eva repeat the two words until she pronounced them to her satisfaction, then she taught her to say, "My name is Eva."

About an hour later, Miss Hughes left, and the lady put the books on the dresser; she was making sandwiches when the man entered the kitchen. They had a brief conversation and agreed something. The lady wrote 'UNCLE STAN' and 'AUNTIE NAN' on a piece of paper; she gave it to Eva and taught her how to say the words, while indicating the name which belonged to each person. After the brief English lesson, Auntie Nan showed her how to brush Meg's and Rusty's fur, and how to carry out simple tasks around the house. Later that morning, she met the boys, who also lived in the farmhouse; they came into the kitchen with Uncle Stan for something to eat. She understood that they were his sons and that their names were Glynn and Tom; she thought they looked about the same age as her brother Iwan. When they went back to work, she had a sleep; when she woke, some children who lived up the lane stopped by to say, "Hello" on their way home from school.

On Saturday morning, she had more lessons with Auntie Nan; she was shown the alphabet book again and taught to say,

'Please and Thank You' and 'My name is Eva, I am six years old.' During the afternoon, Stan, Nancy, and the boys took Eva for a walk across the fields with Rusty and Meg; it was a lovely afternoon, the sun was shining in the pale blue sky and Eva was beginning to feel relaxed in this peaceful valley, where people were kind and unsuspicious. The happy group made their way back to the house when the sun started to disappear behind the hill and the long winter evening approached.

Sunday's misty morning arrived. Eva got out of bed and put on her new red dressing gown and slippers. She drew back the curtains and wiped the condensation off the tiny window with her handkerchief. The sun's gold light swept across the valley and illuminated the naked treetops as they reached skywards through the hovering mist.

She managed to open the window; she could hear sheep in the distance, and saw one of the boys crossing the field with the sheep-dogs. She heard chickens in the yard and birds singing in the woods; all these sounds were new to her. She was used to street noise: angry voices, motor vehicles sounding their horns, and horses and carts rattling by. Red flags with a strange shape printed in the middle hung from buildings; some of the doors had a star crudely painted in yellow, and some people wore a yellow star on their coats.

She went downstairs to the kitchen. Nancy looked up and said, "Bora da, cariad," then, correcting herself, "Good morning, Eva!" After breakfast, they spent a few minutes practicing some of the words and phrases learned the day before.

Nancy finished the jumper; it contrasted nicely with the navy corduroy pinafore. The boys and Uncle Stan came in from the yard, tidied themselves and put on their Sunday best; as it was such a pleasant morning they walked to chapel rather than go in the truck.

Eva didn't understand what was going on. She couldn't remember where she used to pray, only that Papa said they were unable go there anymore; she thought she must be in a synagogue, because people were saying prayers and singing. And yet this place was quite different, the walls were bare, the altar had nothing but a white cloth and a wooden cross on it, and the men wore nothing on their heads. There was a preacher reading from a big book on a stand in front of him – she thought he must be the rabbi.

During the afternoon, a couple of ladies whom Eva had seen at the chapel came to see Auntie Nan. One of them was Mrs. Evans, who thought some of the toys and books Jeannie had outgrown might come in useful. Eva favoured the *Lucie Attwell's Children's Book* ; she found the unusual pictures of the children fascinating.

The other lady gave Eva a brown paper bag; she accepted it and stared at the lady, who nodded with permission to open it. Carefully and suspiciously, she opened the bag and removed a beautiful Fair Isle pixie-hood. Her eyes lit up when she looked at the pretty colours, so intricately entwined in the pattern; she looked across at Nancy. "Put it on," Nancy encouraged. Eva put the hat on, and Nancy lifted her so that she could see herself in the oval mirror above the sideboard; Eva was all smiles.

"Say thank you, Eva," said Nancy.

"Tank Ju," she carefully repeated.

"This is so pretty, I love the colours. Did you knit it?" Nancy asked Mrs. Price.

"Yes, it's an old pattern; I think some of the wool is even older. I remember some of it being in my mother's knitting bag when I was a child. I'm pleased it's been put to good use."

"It certainly has," said Nancy, watching Eva with her new hood on. "Thank you very much, Mrs. Price."

After the ladies were gone, Nancy took Eva outside and showed her how to feed the chickens. Afterwards she took her into the small dairy, where the goats were milked and the cheeses were made. When it started to get dark and cold outside, they returned to the kitchen. Nancy poured everyone a mug of tea from the huge brown teapot, while Stan and the boys sat down to eat their meal.

After dinner, the boys played a game of 'Snap' with Eva. It became boisterous, and Nancy kept her eye on things; she soon saw that Eva understood the game and gave as good as she got. *She's used to teenage boys, by the look of it*, she thought.

Stan was reading his paper unsuccessfully, "Pipe down, you lot! I've read this sentence three times; I can't hear myself think!"

"It's Eva's bedtime now—school tomorrow!" Nancy declared, helping Eva off her chair.

She took Eva to her room, removed the stone hot water bottle from the bed, and tucked her in with Bun the rabbit. *How different this room looks*, she thought, *with the boys' old toy box in the corner, and the teddies and dolls lined up on the shelf.*

Chapter Two

During Friday's assembly, Headmistress Hughes told her pupils that a girl from a land far away was going to join the infants' class. "She is a refugee and has come to Wales to be kept safe at Gorse Wen Farm while her Mammy and Daddy look for a new home."

"Please Miss, what's a refugee?" As usual, Dai Jenkins's hand went up first; he was a bright lad, always asking questions.

"A refugee is someone who left their home because it wasn't safe to live there anymore."

A different hand went up. "Why wasn't it safe, Miss?"

"Well, there could be several reasons: a flood perhaps, or an earthquake, or as in this case, bad men intending to do harm." She left it there, not wanting to worry them unnecessarily.

Dai said, "Miss, will the bad men come here, will we be refugees?"

"No, you're quite safe; those bad men are hundreds of miles away, across the sea in a country called Germany. Look, I'll show you." She went to the world map on the wall and pointed out Germany, and showed them how far it was from Wales.

She continued telling them about Eva, "Your new friend's name is Eva Aarons, and she is six years old; she was put on a train in Germany and travelled to a country called Holland, which is across the sea I've just shown you on the map. She was put on a boat with lots of other children, and it sailed across the water to an English seaside town called Harwich; from there, Eva and some other children came to Wales on another train."

After giving them a moment, she continued, "Eva is going to live with Mr. and Mrs. Morgan at Gorse Wen Farm. Barbara, you live just up the lane and I need you to be a special friend. When you play with Lottie and Joan, I would like you to ask her to join you."

Pleased to have been chosen, Barbara asked, "Miss, Mam says our Michael must look after me when I'm outside, shall we ask him to look after Eva as well?"

"Yes, that's very thoughtful," Miss Hughes looked across the hall for Barbara's ten-year-old brother. "You don't mind doing that, do you, Michael?"

"No, Miss," he replied reluctantly, not wanting another little girl getting in the way of the Cowboy and Indian conflicts with his friends.

To the eldest group of girls, she said, "I'd like a volunteer to support Eva while she's at school because she'll be feeling lost and homesick; I also need that person to help with her English."

The two inseparable friends Mabel and Kathleen had their heads together, whispering as usual. Mabel said, "May we both do it Miss?" Kathleen joined in, "Mabel's used to looking after her sisters, I've only got big brothers so I'd love a little girl to care for."

Miss Hughes considered for a moment. *Two senior girls looking after Eva at school. Why not?* "Yes, girls, you may, thank you."

All the pupils attending the school were present. It was a mixed school with infants starting at the age of five; when they reached seven years of age, they went into the juniors' class, and at eleven, they became seniors. Occasionally a bright student was offered a scholarship, although it was rarely accepted; financial pressure or not wanting to be a white-collar worker were the usual reasons. Even if the parents could afford for the child to stay in education a while longer, it was a very rare occurrence if a child from this village went to the grammar school. Gwen Hughes had been headmistress of the school for fifteen years; during all that time she could only remember three boys fortunate enough to have stayed in education beyond the age of fourteen. She wished there could have been more, because in spite of the Great Depression, all three avoided working in the coal mine and had found good jobs in Cardiff or Bristol.

"Now, children, we'd better get on with our lessons; those of you in Mrs Ward's class, please go to room four; you'll be with me today, because she's poorly. Class 3B, put the homework I gave you on Monday on to the desk in my office, please, and join Mrs Walker's class in room two; she will be teaching you today."

***

There was drizzle in the air on Monday morning when Nancy took Eva to school; they walked along the lane to Felin Fach, the small mill cottage where Madge Lewis lived with her husband and brood of five. Madge's daughter Barbara was in the same class as Eva, and she was going to accompany her.

As they approached the school, Eva had a sense of foreboding. A dark stone building, blackened by coal dust, loomed before her, the leaden sky above emphasising the already grim scene. Her grip on Nancy's hand tightened, and she looked at Barbara, who gave her a reassuring grin.

Miss Hughes was waiting in the entrance porch with a younger teacher; she introduced her colleague. "Good morning, Mrs. Morgan, this is Miss Thompson, the infants' teacher. Eva will be with her for the rest of this year. It will depend on how well she gets on with the language whether or not I get involved; if she does need extra tuition, I'll see she gets it."

Miss Thompson had been Barbara's teacher since the previous year. "Barbara, show Eva where to hang her coat, please; remember, it's the peg with the rabbit on the front, the one I showed you on Friday." While the three adults discussed Eva, Barbara showed her where the infants' coats and hats were kept; there was a row of coat pegs along the wall, each with a different symbol for identification, there were rabbits, stars, kittens, puppies and teddy bears. Some of the pegs already had coats and scarves hanging on them; beneath the coats was a long bench with muddy boots and shoes underneath. They hung their coats on their pegs and returned to the adults.

Nancy was saying goodbye to the teachers; Eva became uneasy, she started to cry and clung to Nancy's skirt. It was hardly surprising the poor little mite was distressed; it was barely a week since her parents had handed her over to the *Kindertransport*. She had travelled halfway across Europe to a place so very different, and on top of all that, there was no one able to explain anything in her own language. Nancy said, "Shall I stay?"

"I think it better you don't; she'll settle in a while," replied Miss Hughes. "Why not leave her with Mrs. Lewis tomorrow morning? She could bring the girls as far as the school gate. I'll look out for them, and keep my distance if Eva seems all right."

Nancy nodded in agreement, "I'll go now, shall I see you this afternoon when I collect her?"

"It's most likely, but if I'm not here, Miss Thompson will be, and she'll tell you how she got on."

Nancy nodded again, she was finding speech difficult because she was trying not to get upset in front of Eva; she said goodbye quickly and left. She remembered how it had been with Tom on his first day, she had cried all the way home and had had a miserable day; she collected him in the afternoon and he was laughing with the other children in the playground. This time was different, though. Tom had been a secure child, and he already knew some of the children. He could speak to them and understand what they were saying, and he understood what the teachers said. What a nightmare for this little girl! *She's only six, perhaps when she's learned more English she'll be all right; the children in her class have only just started learning to read and write. She's not too far behind them.*

Miss Thompson went to her classroom and was settling her pupils while Eva remained with Miss Hughes. She told the children that Eva had arrived and was a bit upset, just as some of them had been last year on their first day. She said they must be very kind and share things with her, especially the sand tray; it was not to turn into the usual battle ground.

Eva was distraught after Nancy's departure, she was panicking because she thought she would never see her again; why was she there, was she going to be sent away again, what is this place? She thought she was going to school, but this wasn't like her kindergarten; it smelled different and everyone spoke in a sing-song way. It wasn't like the hard guttural sound she was used to. All her senses worked against her until she was almost hysterical; Miss Hughes was trying to calm her when she saw the caretaker in the corridor, "Jim, fetch Miss Thompson please, she's in her classroom."

Old Jim, father of eight grown children, noticed Eva's little puddle on the floor and gave the headmistress a knowing look. "Will do! I'll fetch a mop and a bucket as well," he said, as he went to find the other teacher.

Jim told Miss Thompson about the problem, she joined Miss Hughes and Eva with a clean pair of pants in her pocket; she always kept a few socks and underpants in her cupboard, just in case. "Oh dear, had a little accident have we?" she took Eva by the hand and led her into the kitchen where she washed and tidied her. "There now, Eva," she said in a soothing voice. Miss Hughes entered. "How are we doing?"

"All right, she's calmer, but she has no idea what we are saying; it makes it so much more difficult."

"I've an idea. Let's keep Barbara out of lessons this morning; she and Eva can play in my office. I'll do some paperwork and keep an eye on them. Will you go and fetch her please, and bring the wooden carousel with you, along with some crayons and paper."

Miss Thompson returned to her classroom; the children were occupying themselves with the usual high level of noise, she clapped her hands to silence them, "Children, quiet please!" She beckoned Barbara, "You come with me, Barbara, there's something important I need you to do." Addressing the others, she said, "I'll be back in a minute; do some drawing while I'm gone. Peter, you are in charge; quiet as mice, please, children."

On their way to Miss Hughes's office, the teacher explained to Barbara what she wanted her to do, "Play with Eva and keep her busy; show her how the carousel is taken to pieces and put back together again. Do some drawing if you like, and if you want any picture books, ask Miss Hughes, and she'll fetch some for you."

"Here we are," said Miss Thompson brightly, placing toys, wax crayons and paper on the side table. "I'll come back later and see how she's getting on."

Eva, feeling calmer, responded to Barbara's invitation to play. She liked the carousel best; they took it completely to pieces and rebuilt it. She actually laughed when Barbara turned the little handle which made the horses and cockerels move round.

The drizzle had almost stopped when Jim carried the crate of milk into the classroom; he removed two bottles and took them to Eva and Barbara. "The other children are going outside when they've finished their milk," he said helpfully.

"Thank you, Jim, I think these two will be joining them." Miss Hughes smiled up at him. He was such a nice man; she would trust him with her life. Several of his grandchildren were under her care at the school, and not one of them had given her any concerns.

It was pleasant enough for the children to play outside without putting their hats and coats on; some boys played with rugby balls and others joined the girls in their playground games. The first years were holding hands and going round in a circle, singing, 'Ring-a-ring o' roses', and falling down at the end of the rhyme.

Eva stood with Barbara and watched another group of children going round in a circle. They were chanting a different rhyme and changing places with each other; although she hadn't seen that game before, she was more interested in the skipping. There was a long rope with a boy at each end turning it in unison. Two children jumped over the rope at the same time as it skimmed the ground; at a certain point in the rhyme one child left and another entered. She could do that—there was a big skipping rope at her kindergarten.

She wanted to join in, and she looked at the teacher on playground duty, unsure of what to do. The teacher read the expression on Eva's face and sent her to the line of children where she waited her turn. Within moments she was in, skipping in sync with the girl in front. The girl left and someone came in behind Eva—they skipped together until it was Eva's turn to leave. The teacher turned and looked towards Miss Hughes's office; she was standing by the window watching, and gave an approving smile before returning to her desk.

When playtime was over, Barbara took Eva to the classroom. Fear gripped her again when they entered. She looked around the room at the huge clock on the wall, and the stove burning the coal that so many fathers and grandfathers had mined from the hillside. The other children were already seated at their desks, and every one of them was looking at her. In a moment, Miss Thompson was by her side, "Children, this is Eva; say hello." The children greeted Eva as she sat down next to Barbara at the empty desk in the front row. Barbara took hold of her hand, and they were ready to start their lessons.

Miss Thompson read a story about an orphaned boy who lived in London a long time ago; she read excerpts from *Oliver Twist* to her class every day. She knew that Eva would have no idea what she said, but she thought hearing the rhythm of the English language would be advantageous. Afterwards, the children drew with crayons or painted pictures, until the last half hour of the day, which was spent making as much noise as possible with triangles and tambourines. This had been suggested by Mrs. Walker; she was a very experienced teacher who had spent her former years teaching in India, where many of her pupils suffered the effects of trauma. She always found practical lessons best in the early stages: making a noise with musical instruments, plenty of interactive games, and drawing or painting with different colours was the way with such children. Drawing pictures was useful for the teachers too, because it gave an insight into what the child was thinking. "Make a point of looking at Eva's— it should tell you a lot," she suggested.

Miss Thompson wrote the artist's name on the reverse of each picture when they were handed in; one stood out from the rest, because it had been painted in black paint only, the subject being a chapel surrounded by a lot of black crosses. Normally, she wouldn't be too concerned, because the children were at an age where an interest in mortality sometimes starts to creep in. It wasn't unusual for an individual to have a slightly morbid fascination for a while. She read the name, and relief swept over her; the picture of the cemetery had been painted by Sally Thomas. There was no need to be concerned: Sally was a stable child whose granny had recently died. Nevertheless, she thought she would mention it to her mother the next time she saw her.

The other pictures were as expected: some were of the colliery and a bit gloomy, others were farmhouses with sheep in the fields and perhaps a rainbow on the horizon, which wasn't surprising considering the climate. Eva's picture was colourful, with a blue sky and a yellow sun, and a house standing by a tree in a green field; and there were two dogs by a duck pond.

"I didn't expect that," said Mrs. Walker, "it's early days, but it doesn't look as though there's much to worry about here."

"I'll give this to Mrs. Morgan when she comes to collect Eva." Miss Thompson was pleased: after a tricky start, today had turned out much better than expected. The second day was easier, and, by the end of the week, Eva was showing signs of setting into school life.

She was more at ease on the farm, too. Nancy gave her some jobs to do, and let her help look after the chickens; she quite liked them, although she liked the goats best. She asked if she could look after those too. Nancy said, "Not yet; soon, but not yet. They are too boisterous at feeding time and they'll knock you over, when you're a bit bigger you can look after them, and perhaps when the baby ones are born next year you may choose one to keep as a pet." *That should give her something to look forward to*, thought Nancy, *I wish I had some idea how long she's going to be with us. At this rate, leaving here is likely to be another trauma.*

One Saturday morning, a boy from school named Dai came to the farm and asked Eva if she wanted to play, she said she did, but first she must feed the chickens.

"That's all right, I'll help; I like hens," he said. The two young friends went into the small field next to the farmyard where the poultry was kept. The enclosure was large, with a high mesh fence, a third of which was buried in the ground to prevent foxes and other predators digging their way underneath. A quarter of the enclosure was fenced off with a coop roughly in the middle. Young cockerels were fattened in this section before being sent to market. The remaining three quarters of the enclosure housed the best cockerel and his hens; he was very territorial, and likely to attack anyone who entered. Nancy had had her legs pecked many times, and would never go in there without her long boots on. Glynn and Tom avoided it; if any repairs needed doing, they always made excuses saying that there was more important work to do elsewhere. Strangely, with Eva he was less aggressive, and didn't seem to mind her at all.

Nancy had given the fowl some scraps and mash earlier, and let Eva sleep a while longer; she put two buckets of corn feed by the gate for later use, and covered them, to stop the birds and mice stealing the contents. Stan and Nancy watched from the kitchen window as Eva and Dai entered the enclosure; they went into the smaller section first, with a bucket of food for the stock cockerels, and emptied it into the feeding tray; Dai became anxious when the cockerels ran toward them, going mad for the food. Next, they went into the lone cockerel's enclosure. "Just look at her," said Stan, tugging Nan's cardigan. "She's speaking to him!"

'Here, chick, chick' they could hear her saying. "Where's she got that from?" asked Nancy.

"She's got that from you, you talk to them."

"I don't!"

"You do," he laughed. "Look, watch her with that cockerel."

They watched Eva give Dai some food for the hens' tray, then fill a bowl for the cockerel, who was at her side trying to get at it. "Here you are my lovely, here's your dinner," she said, putting the bowl on the ground.

"She's got him eating out of her hand! He's such a nasty blighter, but with her he's a different creature; she's got the makings of a farmer's wife, that's for sure."

"I'm worried about that, she's settling, and still we have no idea how long she will be with us. When the current situation in Germany is over, she'll have to go back and she won't relate to anything over there, not even her own language. I think she was far too young to be sent away."

"Don't worry about it. What are we meant to do, treat her like a lodger, and keep her on the edge of the family? We've had no advice, therefore we'll do it our way. When the time comes for her to go home we'll deal with it; it's what happens to her now that's important." She knew he was right; she felt the same, but she couldn't help worrying.

"We'll collect the eggs while the hens eat their dinner," said Eva. "You hold the basket, and I'll pass them to you, because I know where the hidden ones are." When the eggs were gathered, they tidied the coops, put down fresh water, and returned to the house with the full basket.

Nancy was pleased. "Thank you, you've collected so many; have something to eat when you've washed your hands, then you can go and play outside with Rusty, if you like."

By September, Eva was settled; she understood most of what was said, and her reading and writing was almost equal to that of her classmates. Sometimes she struggled with her spoken words, which caused her some frustration in the classroom, and there were a few tears when she knew she wasn't going to see Mama and Papa for a while, but overall she was happy and doing well, considering her circumstances.

The papers were full of the outbreak of war, and despair swept through the Valleys; it was hard to accept that it was happening again. Stan was worried that his teenage boys might be called up for active service, or sent down the mines to release the stronger men to dig trenches in France and Belgium, as in the previous war.

"What do you think we should tell Eva?" he asked Nancy.

"I think we should say that soldiers from this country are going to fight those bad men in her country, and that it's not going to happen here."

"And her parents and brother?"

"Don't mention them unless she asks; if she does, I think we need to be honest and say we don't know anything at the moment, and we'll tell her when we do."

"Do you think she'll worry?"

"No, I don't, I think she's too young to grasp the seriousness of this," said Nancy, hoping she was right. "We'll deal with any questions as they come along."

Chapter Three

Thoughts of Christmas brought joy to the valley, and lightened the mood; it was something else to think about instead of the gloom and doom in the newspapers. Stalwart farmers coped reasonably well keeping the butcher and greengrocer supplied with meat and produce, the haulier was doing well due to the increased demand for transport of provisions to the towns and cities, and the blacksmith was busy mending almost anything that was broken.

Food unfit for human consumption was used for pig-swill; nothing went to waste, especially clothing. Women were making do and mending, and school girls were taught to knit a garment with wool unravelled from a previously used one. Old clothes were altered—a pair of gents' trousers, shortened to above the knees, and with the waist-band taken in a few inches, became a pair of boy's shorts. An old dress with a worn-out bodice was cut off at the waist and turned into a skirt, or two.

Stan continued to teach Glynn and Tom farm maintenance; some of the men from the village were leaving to join the forces, and demand for their labour was increasing. The papers said that very young men might be conscripted to work in the mines to replace those required for the armed services, and that some women were already working on farms. Stan didn't need any additional help, because he had his two boys; with Nancy's and Eva's input he was coping – just. Glynn was approaching call-up age, although it seemed likely that he would be allowed to continue with what was deemed essential farm work.

This was an exceptionally cold December, and there had been a snowfall already; patches of ice around the farm were a permanent feature, because the sun, now low in the sky, was unable to melt them and dry the puddles. Eva woke early on Sunday morning; her bed was warm and cosy, and she felt like staying there. Nevertheless, she pushed aside the eiderdown and blankets and got out of bed. The room was cold; ice on the inside of the window had formed a beautiful pattern during the night, and the morning sun, shining through, made it sparkle. There were jobs to do before chapel, so she quickly pulled on as many warm clothes as she could and ran downstairs to the kitchen.

"Bora da, cariad," laughed Stan. "Got enough clothes on, have we?" He had risen early and had fired up the range which he had already stoked the night before, and watched with amusement as Eva pulled off her Aran cardigan, her face reddening with the heat.

"Now then, Stan, you know we agreed not to speak any Welsh to Eva, she'll get confused," chided Nancy.

"A little on a Sunday morning won't do any harm, will it my lovely?" he said to Eva, giving her a wink. She chuckled and climbed on to his knee for a cuddle and snuggled into his cushiony tummy before starting to suck her thumb.

"Come on you, you're not a baby!" Nancy said briskly fetching Eva's coat. "Go and get your chores done; the sooner you start, the sooner you'll be finished. When you've done that, have your breakfast and get ready for chapel. This afternoon you may do as you please, as long as you do it quietly."

Eva stood while Nancy turned back the cuffs of the old green coat that someone had kindly donated. "Put your hat on as well, and your thick socks. You're going to need some new wellies with all this snow and ice around." Eva looked comical in the ill-fitting clothes.

Nancy smiled, and said, "I'll get you some new things next week; off you go now. Don't look for eggs, because there won't be any; the hens have stopped laying for a while. Just open the coops, check everything is all right and give them some fresh food and water—and don't be long!"

Eva made her way slipping and sliding across the yard to the enclosure; she opened the outer door and went inside. She opened a coop, not a bird moved. All were settled, and showing no intention of going out in the cold. "Stay there, where it's warm," she instructed. After replacing the stale food and water, she opened all the coops, and locked the enclosure securely when she left.

"She's coming back; don't let her sit on your lap, Stan, she's got to get ready for chapel." Nancy was anxious about the time; everything seemed to take so much longer in the winter.

"You're a hard woman, Nancy Morgan," laughed Stan, pulling on his coat. "I'll go and fetch the boys."

"Yes, do that; be quick, mind. I'll have breakfast on the table before you three turn up."

"Bet you don't."

"I'll bet sixpence I will."

Fewer attended chapel that morning, because ice on the steep pavements made walking difficult. Some older people were worried about falling over and stayed at home, and there were those who lived on isolated farms who didn't want to risk taking a vehicle on to an icy lane. Those who did turn up found the chapel cold and unwelcoming; there was an inefficient stove in the corner, but the small amount of heat it provided was lost in the rafters. Everyone was bundled in dark clothing; their gloves or mittens made turning the hymn books' pages difficult, and most of them had a cold or nasty cough.

The miserable scene was brightened somewhat by Reverend Pritchard's sermon: he spoke of Joseph and Mary's journey to Bethlehem, and added a couple of cheerful carols for good measure. He took a closer look at his congregation: these good people had left their homes on this freezing day. Clearly some should be in a warm bed, but were sticking it out; others appeared anxious to leave and attend to pressing issues elsewhere. Very few looked reasonably comfortable and glad to be among company for an hour on a Sunday morning, especially the two widows whose sons were away in the army.

He was almost finished; he indicated to Mrs. Griffiths at the harmonium that he was ready for her to play 'Oh Come All Ye Faithful.' When the hymn was over, he wrapped the whole thing up ten minutes early and sent everyone home. "Cor, that was heavy going," said Glynn. "I think we need a whip-round for another stove, or else everyone will turn into an atheist!"

"Now then our Glynn, less of that kind of talk on a Sunday," laughed Nancy.

The Morgans didn't do much that afternoon. Stan read his paper and farming magazines again; Tom sorted out his old comics and did some more to his model glider. Glynn and Eva made a scrap-book, and Nancy started to make her plans for the festivities.

Christmas was in the air at school the following day; Eva knew something nice was going to happen, because her friends were getting excited. At chapel yesterday she had understood enough to realise that a baby called Jesus had been born a long time ago, and that she had to praise him—but why had Mr. Price put that small tree branch in the foyer, and why did Miss Thompson talk about making things to put on it? Most importantly, what was a nativity play?

"Hello, little one, what have you been learning today?" asked Nancy when school was over. Eva found it difficult to find the words she needed to ask her questions about Jesus and Christmas. Tom was in the kitchen, so he did what he always did when she was unable to explain something, he got a pencil and paper. She drew a tree branch like the one at school, and a baby in a manger with a star above; he looked at her drawing. "It's a Christmas scene, why would she be confused about that? Don't they have Christmas in Germany?"

"Yes, but Eva is Jewish; I don't know if they celebrate it. Dad might know; he'll be home soon. Tell her the Christmas story, while I make a start on the dinner."

The back door latch clicked and Stan walked in. "Dad, do Jews celebrate Christmas?" Tom asked.

"Search me, why?" replied Stan, peeling off his heavy outer garments and muddy gum boots.

"The school's getting ready for Christmas and Eva seems confused about it."

"I'm not surprised, it confuses me, and I'm not six," joked Glynn.

"I know who to ask: Mrs. Walker. I'll see if I can catch her before lessons tomorrow," said Nancy.

Next morning Nancy and Eva met Barbara in the lane, they walked to school together; Nancy caught sight of the teacher as she crossed the yard. "Mrs. Walker, have you got a moment? Did you come across any Jewish children when you were teaching overseas?"

"Yes, I did. Why, does Eva have a problem?"

"I'm not sure, she doesn't understand Christmas and I wondered if Jewish families celebrate it."

"No, they don't. During December – the dates vary from year to year – they celebrate Hanukkah; it's the eight day Festival of Light. They light a candle each day for eight days, and exchange gifts."

"Thank you, I understand now." Nancy called at the hardware store and bought eight candles. When she returned home, she hid the rest of her shopping on the top shelf of the pantry, arranged the eight candles on a tray, and placed it on the sideboard.

Miss Hughes was near breaking point. Coordinating festivities for almost a hundred children aged between five and fifteen was quite a challenge: there was the carol concert, the nativity play, parties to arrange and decorations to make. The infants were making paper chains, the juniors stars and snow flakes, and the seniors glittery things for the tree branch.

Each class was having its own party; everyone wore their best clothes and took something to eat and drink, if their parents could afford it. The school provided refreshments to make up for those who couldn't. The infants were performing the nativity play; it was always amusing because there was usually an individual who decided to do their own thing on the day. The concert was to be performed by the juniors and seniors. This gave the most concern, because it involved a choir and a band; some children were members of both, and had to quickly move from one to the other during the performance.

Eva's class made the paper chains. Each child was given a pile of different coloured strips of paper and some glue. Most had done this last year, and knew what to do. Dai showed Eva how to make a loop, glue the ends together and thread a different coloured paper through the loop, glue that one and keep going with different colours.

There were paper chains trailing from the desks and on to the floor when Caretaker Jim arrived. "My goodness, you have worked hard, there's enough here to go to the moon and back!" Gathering the chains, he asked, "Who's going to help me put these up?" He chose a couple of volunteers to help him string them across the walls of the classrooms and foyer. When the decorating was finished, Jim took the crib to the foyer; he put some straw in it, and laid models of people and animals next to it, ready for the children to arrange.

What the…? Miss Hughes rose from her desk and closed her office door; the juniors and seniors were rehearsing the concert. *Such a racket, but no doubt it'll all come together in the end,* she thought happily, and with hope.

Miss Thompson chose the actors for the play. Dai was the obvious choice for Joseph, but she didn't pick him; he was going to be one of the kings. Instead, she chose Barry, because she thought playing Joseph might improve his confidence. Mary's part went to Susan, a quiet girl from the mining community, and Eva was to be the peasant girl who gives Jesus a knitted lamb. Everyone was included in the play somehow, even if it was painting the scenery, or singing 'Away In A Manger' at the end.

Christmas was two weeks away, and Nancy's preparations were in full swing; the provisions she had made for the market were in the pantry and ready to go. She had no idea when Hanukkah was this year, so she decided, as this was a Friday, that it would start that evening. She took one of her hidden boxes from the top shelf of the pantry, wrapped it in pretty paper, put it next to the candles on the sideboard, and waited for Eva to arrive home from school.

The boys instantly sensed something in the air, they usually had some sort of fish dinner on Fridays, but this looked as though it was going to be a special occasion, because there was a cloth on the table and the best cutlery was laid.

Eva hadn't noticed the box and candles because she was fussing the dogs. Glynn noticed and asked, "Has Christmas come early?"

"No, it's the start of Hanukkah; well, it is in this house. We're going to celebrate it with Eva, so she won't forget how her people celebrate it."

"Who, but you, would have thought of that?" Stan said, attempting to give his wife a cuddle.

"Oh, go on with you," she said, laughing and freeing herself from his grasp. "All of you, get washed and changed, and then we'll watch Eva light a candle and open her present before dinner."

"What's in the box?" asked Tom.

"Wait and see. Now, will you all get ready for dinner, please!"

While Stan and the boys washed and changed, Nancy showed Eva the tray of candles and the box with her name on it; she instantly recognised the significance, and beamed with joy.

"In a few minutes, you may light the first candle and open your present," said Nancy.

When everyone was ready and gathered in front of the sideboard, Nancy lit a spill and asked Stan to hold the tray of candles; she gave Eva the spill and asked her to choose a candle and light it. The flame settled, and Stan returned the tray to the sideboard. "Should we say a prayer or something?"

"I suppose we should," replied Nancy, looking at Eva for a reaction; there was none so she gave her the box to open. She tried to unwrap it without tearing the paper, "Come here, like this," said Tom ripping it off. "You're supposed to tear it, that's half the fun!"

"I could have used that again," laughed Nancy.

Eva opened the box: inside was a beautiful doll with curly brown hair. Her eyes opened and closed, and she wore a bright pink polka dot dress, white lace socks and shiny black shoes. Eva fell in love with her instantly, and, in a second, the doll was out of the box and in her arms. "Oh, thank you! I love her."

"Come on, let's eat, we're having special fish and chips tonight, made by me!" said Nancy.

When Eva's candle burned low, Nancy said it was time for bed, because both of them had a very busy day tomorrow. Eva kissed everyone goodnight and carefully carried her doll upstairs; it was in the bed next to her when Nancy went to tuck her in.

"I love my dolly," Eva said sleepily.

"I'm glad, has she got a name yet?"

"Babs."

"Babs, is it? That's a very modern name, where've you heard that before?"

"It's short for Barbara; her mama won't allow her to be called Babs so we only say it when she's not there—but you mustn't say anything."

"Oh, I won't, not if it's a secret." Trying not to laugh, Nancy said, "Shall we sit Babs on the chair until morning?" Eva was sleepy, and made no objection when the doll was removed from the bed; she was fast asleep by the time it was seated on the chair.

Chapter Four

After the horrible weather of the past week, it was a pleasure to get up early and go outside. The sun was rising over the hills, and the sky was cloudless; it was going to be a beautiful day. Stan and the boys had breakfasted and were already outside, intending to take advantage of the good weather and get as much work completed as possible, in case the weather turned against them in the new year.

When Eva was dressed, Nancy explained what they were going to do that day. "This morning we're going to make decorations like the ones at school; I'll cut out some shapes to start you off, then you can continue on your own."

While Nancy stirred the bowl of gingerbread mixture, she glanced across at Eva, and wondered if she ought to have given her the glitter because it was going all over the floor where the dogs were lying; she knew she'd be weeks getting rid of it.

Stan went into the woods to cut some small branches of laurel to make the tree. By the time he got back, Eva and Nancy were ready to start decorating it. "I'll go and get a bucket to stand the tree in, then I'll go into the loft for the decorations," he said. "Tom has told me that me he wants to decorate the tree with Eva."

"That's all right, he can do that. I've plenty of other things to get on with," Nancy said, wondering what to do first.

During the afternoon, Stan passed the box of decorations to Tom. "Here you are; throw out any tatty ones, and be sure to use those Eva made this morning. There's some gingerbread men as well, hang them high up so Rusty and Meg can't get at them."

Stan took Nancy out of the room, and whispered, "I'm going to be dealing with the poultry on Sunday, how do you think Eva will react?"

"Badly, I should think; she won't understand, and it's bound to be distressing for her, she ought not to be here really. Give chapel a miss this week and make a start while we're there. I think I'll ask Madge if she can play with Barbara afterwards." When Madge heard what was happening at the farm, she said Eva could have her dinner with them and stay there until the job was done.

On Sunday afternoon Nancy went to Felin Fach to collect her, "Thank you Madge, we've finished and the birds are ready to go, I'll explain it all to her on the way home."

As expected Eva was very upset; she had fed those chickens for weeks, and was attached to them. In an attempt to cheer her, Nancy asked her to help sort out the provisions for the market. "I'll pass them down to you, and you put them on that shelf." Eva tearfully took the Christmas cakes and puddings from Nancy, and stacked them on the shelf next to the jars of chutney and jam.

"Good girl, it's almost your bedtime now; wash your hands and face, and brush your teeth. I'll be up in a minute to tuck you in and read you a story." Nancy took Glynn's old Winnie-the-Pooh book from the book case, and went upstairs to Eva's room.

Eva was in bed, cuddling Bun and sucking her thumb, "All right, love?" she asked gently, saddened to see their little angel so upset.

"I don't want any Christmas dinner; I'll just have potatoes and gravy, please," Eva said mournfully.

"Just potatoes and gravy? All right, what about some pudding afterwards?"

"I think I'd like to have the pudding."

"In that case, you shall. Now, how do you fancy a story about Winnie-the-Pooh, you like him, don't you?"

Eva nodded and snuggled down still clutching the rabbit and sucking her thumb. After two paragraphs, she was gone, fast asleep. Nancy tucked her in, kissed her cheek, and went downstairs.

The week before Christmas flew by: the nativity play, the carol concert and the parties were successful, and everyone who attended said that they had thoroughly enjoyed them.

Stan and the boys were still working flat out on the farm; the walling and fencing repairs were finished on the lowland, and Glynn and the two dogs brought the sheep down from the hills and put them in one of the fields, where they were to stay until lambing was complete in the spring.

In no time at all, it was Christmas Eve, and time to wind down. "Will you light a fire in the front room, please, Stan? It could do with airing before tomorrow," said Nancy.

"We're not going in there are we? It's not very cosy, and the three-piece is as hard as nails."

"We can't spend Christmas Day in the kitchen!"

"Why not? We eat in here every other day of the year; why do we have to go in there?"

"Because it's our best room, and Christmas Day is special."

"There's nothing to do in there, all our things are in here."

"Oh, for heaven's sake, Stan, it's only for one day, we can take things in there to amuse us."

"The boys won't want to be in there, and neither will Eva. The table's in the kitchen, and we'll need it if we want to play cards or start the new jigsaw. And anyway, the kitchen will be much warmer after all that cooking."

Seeing she was going to be outnumbered, and that he did have a good argument for staying in the kitchen, she gave in. "All right, but if anyone drops in on us we're going in the front room—so please light that blasted fire!"

Glynn and Tom went out for the evening with their friends. Eva went to bed early, because she thought doing so would make the morning come quicker. Before she went, Stan put a glass of sherry and a mince pie on a tray for Santa, and a chopped carrot on a saucer for the reindeer. "These will keep them going while they deliver the presents all around the world," he explained. "Let's put them on the mantlepiece in the front room."

Confused, she asked, "How will they find it?"

"Santa will come down the chimney when he delivers your presents—don't worry, he'll see it."

"But there's a fire there, he'll get burned."

"No, he won't, because I'm going to put the fire out before he arrives. Look, I've let it burn low, it's almost out now; he won't get burned, I promise."

Satisfied, she followed him into the front room where he put the tray on the mantelpiece. "Come on, then; if you want to go to bed this early, would you like me to read to you tonight, or shall I fetch Auntie Nan?" She said she wanted him to read the story this time. When she was fast asleep, he returned to the front room; he drank the sherry, ate the mince pie, and put the empty glass on the tray, making sure there were some crumbs left. He removed the pieces of carrot, and joined Nancy in the kitchen. "I could drink another sherry, would you like one?"

"Yes, come on, let's sit down and relax while we can," she replied, fetching the sherry bottle and two glasses.

"I'm glad we're staying in here; it's much cosier with the smell of the spices and all." He sank into his old leather chair and put his feet on the fender. "It's a joy to be warm; the winters really get into my bones these days."

"It's barely started. I reckon it'll be a hard one this year, and with plenty of snow, I shouldn't wonder. Thank goodness we've none at the moment, although it's going to be frosty tonight; the ground was already glistening when I went outside."

"What time are you expecting the boys?" asked Stan, looking at the clock. It was half past nine; he had been up well before daybreak, and was tired.

"I told them to be back by ten o'clock; do you want to go to bed?"

"Yes, but I want you to come up with me; it's going to be a busy day tomorrow, with an early start."

"All right, let's get ready; where shall we put the presents?" she asked.

"I think in the front room by the fireplace, don't you? Eva will think Santa put them there; when she's seen them we can bring them in here and open them in the warm."

"Good idea, I'll get them; will you look in on her while I do that, please?" Stan did as she asked, and carefully opened Eva's bedroom door. Meg was lying at the foot of the bed; her tail started to thump on the linoleum floor when she saw her master. "Shush, come here," he whispered, when he saw that Eva was fast asleep.

Nan looked up from sorting the presents when he returned. "She's fine; Meg was guarding her. She's got a way with animals; I think we should consider getting her a pet of her own soon."

"What have you got in mind? I did say she could choose one of the kids and keep it as a pet, although she might be going home before long, because there doesn't seem to be much happening on the war front. Mrs. Price said she'd heard that most of the English evacuees in the Rhondda had been sent home for Christmas, and wouldn't be returning."

"Don't you be too sure; I've heard there's plenty going on in Poland. Just because the papers aren't reporting much, it doesn't mean there's nothing going on. Hitler's not likely to stop now, unless he's forced."

"Let's see what happens. She can have some chicks in the spring if she's still here, and she can have a goat; I think that'll be enough for now. Perhaps when one of the cats produces a litter she can look after the one we keep, but I do think we need to be very careful— this worries me."

"I know, you're right," Stan said reluctantly. He wanted to give Eva a puppy, and perhaps a pony the following year, but he thought it best not to mention it.

"Come on, let's go up; it's almost ten o'clock, the boys can let themselves in."

By five o'clock on Christmas morning, Tom, Nancy, and Stan were up. As Nancy had predicted, there had been a heavy frost; everywhere from the cwm to the hills was sparkling in moonlight.

"Oh my, what a wonderful sight! Happy Christmas, cariad," Stan said, giving Nancy a quick peck on the cheek.

"Happy Christmas, son," he said, turning to Tom and shaking his hand. At almost fifteen years of age, he still rose early on Christmas mornings, unlike Glynn two years his senior, who preferred a lie in.

"Come on, Tom, let's do all the outside jobs this morning, so Mam can get on with what she needs to do."

"Try and be quiet, because if Eva wakes early, none of us will get anything done," said Nancy, secretly willing her to wake.

An hour later, Stan and Tom returned with more logs and coal, "Can we do anything?" asked Stan.

"Yes, please, the range needs stoking and there's the potatoes and carrots to peel," Nancy said. *What a treat, to have someone to peel potatoes for me.*

When Eva woke, she remembered it was Christmas Day; she got out of bed quickly, pulled on some clothes and ran down the stairs.

By seven o'clock, there was still no sign of Glynn. "Do you remember when the boys were little, and they woke us up at half past three in the morning?" asked Stan.

"I do; we all fell asleep in the afternoon!" Nancy turned to Eva. "Go and wake Glynn; tell him Santa's been and we're going to open our presents in a minute."

She ran upstairs and jumped on to Glynn's bed, "Wake up, or you won't get any presents!" She ran down as quickly, in case they started without her. Moments later, Glynn emerged, half asleep in his pyjamas and dressing gown.

Eva helped Tom and Glynn carry the presents into the kitchen; they all sat by the range and took it in turns to open their gifts. Eva was first. Stan gave her a jigsaw puzzle of a harbour scene with boats, shops and warehouses. A horse and cart were parked on the quay. She loved it. Nancy suspected that Stan wanted to help her do it because it was far too difficult for a child of her age; there were seven hundred and fifty pieces. He really had no idea sometimes! The boys gave her a cot for Babs, which they had made between them. Nancy said that after Christmas she would cut up an old sheet and make some bedding for it.

Nancy and Stan gave her a new blue coat and shiny black wellington boots; Nancy knitted her a hat, scarf and mittens, all matching in pale blue and navy wool. She had also knitted three pairs of socks, two grey pairs, and one white pair for best; with the left over white wool she made a twin set for Babs.

Eva gave everyone the gifts she made at school. She gave the boys a glittery Christmas card each; she made a handkerchief for Stan with a wonky 'S' stitched in the corner; and for Nancy she made a needle case of yellow felt with an 'N' childishly stitched on the front.

Opening the presents took a long time, and Nancy was anxious to get on with the meal. Stan had been right as usual, and she was pleased that he had persuaded her not to use the front room, otherwise she'd have been stuck in the kitchen on her own, and missing all the fun.

When they were all seated for dinner, Nancy put the large roasted chicken on the table. Stan started to carve, while Nancy put the vegetables and trimmings on to the plates. She passed each one to Stan, for him to put plenty of meat on. She passed Eva a small plate, with only potatoes and gravy on it, and gave Stan a wink; Eva took her plate and looked at it. She looked up at Nancy, and at her plate again.

"You said you wanted only potatoes and gravy," said Nancy, pretending to be serious. She waited a moment, "All right, I take it you want some meat after all? Come on then, pass your plate to Uncle Stan and he'll give you some chicken."

Although this had been a comical moment for Nancy, she was relieved; livestock farming was a tough life. She knew all about that. She had been a teacher before she became a farmer's wife, and memories of when Stan had taught her how to kill and prepare a chicken, as well as the first time she had seen the lambs go to market were still very clear in her mind. Eva was a city child, and her early life was totally different to those of children brought up on farms, but she would learn and come to terms with seeing animals raised for food. When she went home to her family, the time spent here on the farm and at school in the village would have given her experiences no city child was likely to have. She felt a slight pang of guilt, knowing that she had given a Jewish child non-kosher food; but Eva didn't know, and she had enjoyed it.

When dinner was over, Eva played on the floor with the dogs and her toys, while Stan and the boys did the washing up, and Nancy put everything away. Later in the afternoon, they gathered around the table and played a few board games. At tea time, they were still full after their dinner, and no one wanted anything to eat. The fire in the front room had made the room more welcoming, so they went in there for the evening and sang songs to Nancy's accompaniment on the piano.

Chapter Five

According to Eva's identity papers, her seventh birthday was due in February; it was her first since she had arrived at the farm. Although they were in the middle of lambing, the Morgans wanted to make it special.

"Would you like a birthday party?" Nancy asked.

"Could I have Dai and Barbara come to tea instead of a party?"

"Of course, you don't have to have one if you'd rather not; I'll make a special tea and you can play together afterwards. Have you any idea what you would like for a present? Uncle Stan and I were wondering if you would like some chickens of your own, and perhaps a rabbit."

Eva liked the idea, especially when Glynn and Tom said that they would section off a part of the enclosure and build a coop just for her hens. Stan said that he would take her to the livestock market and help her choose some in the spring.

Nancy was troubled when Eva's birthday arrived, because there was no word from her parents, "It's not that I think she expected anything; in fact I doubt she's given it a thought, but it's so sad, isn't it? Goodness knows how the Aarons are feeling," she said to Stan.

"I can't imagine; it's an awful situation. At least with an English evacuee, the parents know where the child is, or at least have an address. Eva's parents have no idea where she is. It's a complete and utter nightmare."

"She must be feeling something, surely? This time last year, she was with them. I'll keep a close eye on her; I'm pleased it's half term and she'll be here with us today."

Eva spent most of the morning with the boys; in the afternoon she helped Nancy prepare for her guests. Dai arrived at around three o'clock, and Barbara arrived not long after.

Nancy lit the candles on Eva's cake and watched with Stan while Dai instructed, "Blow them out, and make a wish at the same time." After tea, Glynn and Tom played games with the children; when it began to get dark, they took Dai and Barbara home, while Nancy and Stan tidied the room. "This has been the best birthday I've ever had!" declared Eva.

"Did you make a wish?" asked Stan.

"Yes, I wished I could live here for ever."

"You're not supposed to say what you wished for; you're meant to keep it to yourself," explained Nancy.

"That's silly! If you don't tell, no one will know what you want," replied Eva.

"She's got a point," laughed Stan.

On St. David's Day, women from the village made the Bethesda Chapel's altar look festive with leeks and early daffodils. The Morgans attended the evening service, and Glynn sang in the choir. Eva was dressed in full national costume, along with the other girls. Their red and black skirts, crisp white blouses and black felt hats made a cheerful sight.

She had enjoyed today; at school she had learned about Saint David and his mother Saint Non, and where they lived in Pembrokeshire, a very long time ago. She made two crepe paper daffodils, for herself and Nancy, and small felt leeks for Stan, Glynn, and Tom, which they wore on their lapels.

It's happy, I am, thought Eva, after they finished singing the second hymn. *I hope my wish comes true.* "Auntie Nan," she whispered, "Mama, Papa, and Iwan could come and live in Wales, couldn't they?"

"Shush, we'll see." *Oh dear God...* thought Nancy.

Spring arrived; daffodils and primroses growing wild in the woods and along the verges were a welcome sight as the days grew longer. Lambing was over for another year, and the sound of bleating was heard throughout the valley. Stan's flock was taken to the high ground, to enable the field to recover after winter grazing.

Some of Nancy's nannies had given birth, and, as promised, Eva was allowed to choose one; she already knew which one she wanted because she had watched it being born. It was a weakling at first, but after a couple of days it rallied, and at two weeks it reached its proper weight. She chose a female, because she wanted to milk it and make produce like Auntie Nancy; she named it Grace because it was completely white, and trotted around daintily.

The local livestock market was on Wednesdays, which meant they had to wait until the Easter holiday before Stan could take her. Nancy thought there should be some chicks for sale by now. "Take her with you, and let her choose the ones she wants."

"All right, we could do with some fresh stock as well," he replied.

"She wants Bantams. She's been looking at the pictures in your magazines; she likes those because they're smaller," said Nancy.

"Bantams! She doesn't want Bantams! There's no meat on them. She wants bigger, meatier birds. Bantams are neither useful, nor ornamental."

"Stan, do you think for one moment that Eva wants a flock of hens to fatten and sell at market for meat? She's seven years old, she wants them as pets."

"Well, it's her birthday present; perhaps when she sees some of the other breeds she'll change her mind," he said hopefully.

On market day morning Eva rose early, after Glynn and Stan loaded six lambs into the trailer, they were ready to go. They rattled down the bumpy lane and turned left, on to the main road, "Ten green bottles hanging on a wall…" sang Stan as he drove up the hill.

"Ten green bottles hanging on a vall," continued Eva.

"Wall," corrected Stan, "and if one green bottle should accidentally fall, there'd be nine green bottles hanging on the…?"

"Vall."

They arrived at the market, and Stan took the lambs to the auctioneer; when the paperwork had been dealt with, he took Eva to the pens where the other animals were kept. It was a noisy place; the animals made a lot of noise, and so did the farmers, talking in groups and putting the world to rights. The clanking of the metal gates when the pens were opened and closed echoed around the huge barn. Eva didn't like it and wanted to leave. "Not long now," said Stan. "Our lambs will be in the ring soon; let's go and look at the poultry and rabbits while we wait."

He took her to see some regular farmyard hens. "Are these Bantams, Uncle Stan?"

"Er, no, but they are very good layers,"

"Where are the Bantams?" she asked. Stan found the man selling the poultry, and asked him if he had any Bantams.

"I have, but there's not much choice—no call for 'em, you see. I've got some over here." He took them to the cages of

Bantams, Eva peered into the cages as though she knew what she was looking for.

"For the little girl, are they?" he asked, noticing Stan was standing back.

"Yes, her first flock; it's a birthday present."

"Help you choose some, shall I?" the man offered Eva. Turning to Stan, he asked, "How many is she to have?"

"Ten to start with, and one cockerel," replied Stan. Eva chose the ones she wanted, and they were put into a holding cage while the lambs were auctioned. All were sold for a satisfactory price, and, with the auction out of the way, they went to the truck to fetch the cages for Eva's birds.

On the way home, they had another try with Ten Green Bottles; by the time there were no bottles left on the wall, Eva was just about able to sing 'wall' instead of 'vall'.

When they returned to the farm, they carried the cages to her section of the poultry enclosure. Nancy stopped what she was doing and joined them. "Let them go, Eva, let's have a look at them," she said.

Eva released the birds and they ran around the pen, happy to be free after being caged for hours. "Beautiful birds, Eva," remarked Nancy. "Did you pick them yourself?"

"I did, except the cockerel; the man at the market helped me, he said he had one which would be perfect for me."

Stan said, "He was most helpful; he knows his birds."

Nancy looked closer at the young male; the colours of his feathers were vibrant with a metallic lustre. "Oh, I love him! Isn't he beautiful, Eva?"

"His name is Iwan. I've named some of his wives: that one is Mary; the one in the corner is Ruby; those three pecking the ground are Wendy, Kathy, and Ethel. Barbara is over there with Helga; I've just got to find three more names."

Within a few weeks, Eva's hens were old enough to start laying eggs. She was excited when she found the first one, and ran into the house with it, "May I have it for breakfast, please?" she asked Nancy.

"Of course, fried or poached?" she asked.

"Fried, please."

"Fried it is, then; go and wash your hands while I cook it."

Eva washed her hands and sat at the table, while Nancy made her egg on toast. "Look, you've got a double yolker; we don't see many of those, do we?"

At the beginning of May, Tom found a litter of kittens among the brambles at the foot of a tree. He was working in the woodland when he noticed one of the cats creeping into the undergrowth. He stopped working and peered through the leaves. She was lying on her side, suckling four kittens. His first instinct was to leave them where they were, and let nature take its course; his second was to move them to safety, because they were easy prey when she left them to find food for herself.

Sometimes there were too many cats having kittens on the farms; at other times, demand outstripped supply. He was certain he would find homes for all these; they needed at least one more themselves. There was scant arable land in the area, and animal feed had to be brought in from other parts of the country at a cost. Vermin was an expensive problem, so he decided to move them to the safety of a barn. He stopped what he was doing and went to the barn where the machinery was kept. After he had found a box and lined it with old newspaper, he went to find Nancy. "Mam, I've found a litter of kittens in the woods; will you help me move them, please?"

She followed him to where the cat and kittens were, she trampled down the brambles and crouched beside them.

"We must be quick so that she doesn't reject them. I'll pass you the kittens and you take them to the barn; I'll follow with the mother." Nancy picked up the first kitten and handed it to Tom; the mother looked anxious, so she quickly passed the remaining three to him and said, "Go, don't wait for me, I'll catch up with you." She gently picked up the cat, who was beginning to show signs of distress. She was able to walk faster than Tom because he was carrying the box of kittens; she caught up with him, and, within moments, they were in the barn.

Tom put the box under the bench, and Nancy placed the mother in the box with her kittens; she settled instantly and began to lick them. "They'll be all right. Now, what have we got? A black and white, and three tabby and white; they look healthy enough, about a couple of days old I reckon. Lucky you found them when you did. I don't think they would have lasted long out there."

Dai was with Eva when she arrived home from school; they were going to play for a while until tea time. Nancy told them about the kittens. "Come and see them!" They followed her to the barn where the cat was resting with her four babies by her side, all piled on top of each other, fast asleep.

"There's four, look; the black and white one is easy to see. The other three blend in with each other, although one does have a white tip on its tail."

"Can I hold one?" asked Dai.

"Yes, but not today, because they're asleep, and it's a bit too soon; you may hold one in a few days when they're stronger and moving around," said Nancy.

The following week Dai returned to the farm to see the kittens, and, as Nancy had promised, he held them. Eva favoured the black and white male; his eyes were still closed, and he mewed for his mother when he was lifted from the nest, "It's all right, Dai. Hold him gently for a moment; he'll make a much better pet if he's handled early. He must get used to humans while he's still a baby," explained Nancy.

"Would you like one of the kittens, Dai?" asked Eva.

He shook his head sadly. "I asked Dad if I could have one. He said no because there's enough strays hanging around as it is. But they aren't like these, they're old and tatty and they fight."

"Well," said Eva, stroking the top of the kitten's head while he held it, "you can share mine. I shall call him Dai, after you."

Nancy said, "He shall be known as 'Dai the cat' and you will be 'Dai the boy.' Put him back with his brother and sisters for now, and next time you come you may hold him again."

In September, Eva moved with the other juniors into Mrs. Walker's class. She liked her, even though she was very strict, and was quick to rap a ruler across the knuckles of naughty children.

Three girls evacuated from Liverpool joined them; the Luftwaffe had recently bombed the city and there was concern for the safety of the children living there.

On their way to school one morning, Eva and Barbara saw Helen Bates, one of the evacuees, walking towards them. They greeted her, and asked why she was going in the opposite direction. "I'm running away," she replied. "I'm going home."

"Home? How will you get there?"

"I'm going to hitch-hike; please don't tell anyone," pleaded Helen, as she left them and continued to walk along the main road.

When the children were at their desks and ready to start lessons, Mrs. Walker called the register:

"Susan Andrews?"

"Yes, Miss."

"John Atkins?"

"Here, Miss."

"Helen Bates?"

No reply.

"Helen Bates?"

Mrs. Walker looked up, saw that Helen's desk was vacant, and marked her absent. Barbara started to cry. "Shut up, you'll give the secret away," Eva said sternly. They thought no more about Helen until that evening.

Her guardians went to Miss Hughes's house after she failed to return home from school. They all went to Mrs. Walker's to ask if Helen had been in school that day; she confirmed that she had not. Fear and panic was rising. Miss Hughes asked Mrs. Walker, "Has she made any friends? Who is she closest to?"

Mrs. Walker tried to think. "Eva Aarons and Barbara Lewis seem to be the closest to her."

"Let's go to Gorse Wen first; if we draw a blank we'll go to Felin Fach," said Miss Hughes.

Eva was in her bedroom when she heard a knock on the front door and a familiar voice: "I'm sorry to disturb you, Mr. Morgan— one of the evacuees was absent from school today and she's missing, we need to speak to Eva please."

"Come inside," Stan said, and went to fetch Eva. Miss Hughes explained why they were there and asked if she knew anything.

"She's run away," Eva informed them with a matter of fact tone.

"Good God, child! What do you mean she's run away?" exclaimed Stan in disbelief.

"She's gone to Liverpool; she's going to hitch a lift."

"Hitch a lift, who from?"

"Lorry drivers," said Eva, as though he was missing the obvious.

The adults felt ill. An eight-year-old girl could not hitch-hike from the Welsh Valleys to the Port of Liverpool without serious risks. "Thank you, Mr. Morgan; we'll contact the police," said Miss Hughes.

The frantic adults went to the police house and remained there while the constable sent out an alert. Before long the telephone rang; it was the police at Buith Wells. She had just arrived, and was safe with them.

After Eva and Barbara spoke to her in the morning, Helen had hitch-hiked along the main road; eventually a lorry driver took her to Brecon and dropped her off there. She continued walking for a considerable time, until a man in a delivery van heading for Buith Wells saw her. He stopped, and asked where she was going; she said that she needed a lift to Liverpool. Thankfully, he was alert; he offered her a lift to Liverpool, which she accepted. As soon as he reached Buith Wells, he took her to the police station and handed her over to the duty officer.

"Bloody hell!" declared Stan when he heard the outcome, "That idiot driver that took her to Brecon! Did he not realise the girl was eight years of age? What was he thinking?"

Nancy said, "Goodness knows! Good job the second driver cottoned on; I dread to think what could have happened to that child. Liverpool is about two hundred miles away. She could have died of exposure out there during the night. My legs go weak just thinking about it."

Miss Hughes sent for Eva and Barbara the following morning, and told them that Helen had been found, "What I don't understand is, why didn't you say something when Mrs. Walker marked her absent, you knew where she was and where she was going, didn't you?"

Eva spoke, "Miss, Mama said if anyone told me a secret, I must never tell."

Gwen Hughes paused, *Just when I thought I'd heard and seen it all*. "Eva and Barbara, in the interest of others, there are times when you must consider the situation and tell someone. Do you understand what I am saying?"

"Yes, Miss," they mumbled, before their head mistress dismissed them.

Chapter Six
1945

The war ended when Eva was twelve. She had mastered her difficulty pronouncing Js and Ws, and her schoolwork was equal to most. During the previous six years, some of the boys working at the foundry down at the coast had been sent to the colliery to replace those men sent into active service; some of the younger women and teenage girls either replaced the boys or joined the Land Army.

Glynn and Tom were allowed to continue working with Stan, as long as the farm's output reached government requirements; some of their lowland pasture had been ploughed for growing root vegetables, and the number of sheep had been increased, to provide more wool for the forces' uniforms, and meat for the general public. Nancy worked on the farm alongside her menfolk, and Eva was expected to do more housework after school and at weekends.

Most families in the area came through the war relatively unscathed, although Dai's brother Martin was killed in France, and there were a few others who didn't return.

Eva's self-appointed mentors, Kathleen and Mabel, had left school during the war. Mabel was one of the typists in an office in Port Talbot, and was waiting for her fiancé to be demobbed. Kathleen stayed in the village and worked in the bakery; she was going steady with Mick, one of the haulier's sons.

Eva's friendship with Barbara strengthened, and they were very close. Dai had been a special friend too. They used to spend hours playing together or roaming the hills with Rusty; but gradually he became sidelined, when Eva and her friends found clothes and American films more interesting than playing in fields and building dens in woodland.

Post war recovery was the priority across Europe. Major clearing operations were taking place, and bomb sites turned into children's playgrounds; perpetrators of war crimes were being arrested, and British and Allied troops were in Germany, managing the infrastructure. Information about the Holocaust, its victims and other missing persons was being compiled, and survivors were searching for family and friends.

There had been no contact with Eva's parents. The authorities were searching for them, along with the thousands of other displaced people. In the meantime she was to continue living with the Morgans. She was anxious about the prospect of leaving, because Gorse Wen Farm was her home now. Her memories of Mama and Papa were shadowy; she had forgotten how to speak her limited German, and she never had learned to read or write it.

At the close of 1946, information about Iwan reached Stan and Nancy. They learned that he had died of typhoid in a labour camp during 1941. They decided not to tell Eva yet, because it was looking likely that the lists of death camp victims would reveal the fate of her parents before long.

When Eva was fourteen, and in her final year at school, her classmates were deciding what they wanted to do when they left. There were plenty of jobs for everyone, and it was just a matter of choice, or capability. She wanted to work in the haulier's office, although it didn't seem likely that she would be allowed to, because of her present status. New businesses were being established; the animal feed and hardware store expanded, and the hairdresser, who used to do the 'shampoo and sets' in her customers' homes during the war opened a new salon in the village.

During March, written confirmation concerning the fate of Eva's parents arrived. It revealed that Ike and Frieda Aarons had died in Belzec extermination camp in 1942. It also confirmed Eva's new status in the United Kingdom, and several forms requiring completion were enclosed.

Stan and Nancy found this too onerous to deal with alone, and decided to involve Miss Hughes. Nancy went to the school and gave her the documents for perusal. They agreed not to tell Eva yet, but to meet after school the following day to discuss the situation.

On the way home, she called at Felin Fach to tell Madge the sad news; Madge said that Eva could have her tea with them while they were in the meeting.

Having read the documents, Miss Hughes was prepared for her meeting with Stan and Nancy; they looked anxious when they entered her office. She stood, and, with tears in her eyes, said, "This is a very sad outcome indeed."

"Aye, it's a rum do, God love her," replied Stan.

"Please, sit down," she encouraged. "This appears quite straightforward. Eva has no known surviving next of kin; therefore she will remain in the United Kingdom. Because she's a minor, she requires a legal guardian and a permanent residence. She will become a British citizen, which means that her status will be equal to that of anyone else her age as far as the British Government is concerned."

"Stan and I would like to apply for guardianship, and have her continue to live with us," Nancy said hopefully.

"That will merely be a formality, I'm sure. I'll support your application, and I know Reverend Pritchard will too. The most pressing issue at the moment is to tell Eva what's happened to her family."

Stan asked, "Do you think it should be done here, or at the farm?"

"I think at the farm," replied Miss Hughes. "Would you like me present when you tell her?"

"I think I would," replied Nancy, glancing toward Stan for agreement.

"In that case, I'll be there; she may need a few days off school, but, on the other hand, she might want to be with her friends."

Nancy was keen to get this done as quickly as possible. "How soon will you be available?"

"I can be there at eight o'clock tomorrow morning. I think the sooner the better, don't you?" Miss Hughes gathered the documents and handed them to Stan. "If you need any assistance completing these forms, just ask."

"We will, thank you; we'll see you about eight o'clock tomorrow."

As soon as they arrived home, Stan went to find Glynn and Tom, they entered the kitchen and Nancy told them. "We have news of Eva's family: her parents died in an extermination camp five years ago, and her brother died of typhoid in a labour camp the previous year. Miss Hughes will be here at eight o'clock tomorrow morning while we tell her."

"Where is she now?" asked Glynn.

"She's at Felin Fach with Barbara; she'll be home soon."

"How did her parents die?" asked Tom.

"They were gassed," said Nancy. "We're not going into any details with her at the moment, unless she asks; we're just going to tell her they died, and that she'll be staying here and not returning to Germany."

"That should be a relief; she didn't want to go back there anyway," said Tom.

"At least the uncertainty's gone; she can settle now," added Glynn.

Everyone was up early; Glynn and Tom ate their breakfast and left the house. Stan returned after completing his early chores, and Nancy was all nerves.

Miss Hughes arrived while Eva was upstairs getting ready for school, "Where is she?" she asked in a low voice.

"Upstairs; she'll be down in a minute."

When Eva entered the kitchen, she was surprised to see her head mistress sitting with Stan and Nancy at the table; she could tell by their faces that something was wrong. At first she thought she was in trouble, she looked at each one in turn and quickly realised what this could mean.

Stan said, "Sit down, Eva; we must to talk to you."

She was told as much as they felt she needed to know; she was quiet and didn't ask any questions. Nancy reassured her that she was going to stay with them, and that she would be able to work in the village when she finished school. Eva nodded and said nothing.

Miss Hughes said, "Don't go to school for the rest of this week unless you want to. I'll tell your friends. Would you like me to ask Barbara to come to see you after school today?"

Eva nodded, "Yes please, Miss."

"All right then, I'll see you on Monday, unless you want to go back before."

Nancy saw Miss Hughes to the door, "Thank you for your support; it is appreciated."

"If there's anything I can do, you know where I am. Perhaps, one day next week, if you're passing, you could call in and we'll have a chat."

"Thank you, I will," said Nancy.

"I'll give you a lift home, if you like; I've got to get some more feed from the village," said Stan, putting on his coat.

"That's most kind. Thank you."

"All right?" Stan asked of Nancy. "I won't be long." He gave Eva a pat on her shoulder, and left with Miss Hughes.

"Do you feel like any breakfast?" asked Nancy. Eva shook her head, and remained silent. Nancy sat beside her while they drank their tea; tears started to run down Eva's face. Nancy put her hand on her arm. "Let it go, Eva; you must grieve." Eva sobbed, and so did Nancy.

"It looks as though Uncle Stan is back," said Nancy, watching him unload the feed into the barn. "Let's have something to eat with him. When he's gone back to work, we can go for a walk if you like; it'll do us both good."

Eva and Nancy walked down the lane as far as the ford and across the adjacent field, and as they walked along the sheep track, Nancy talked to Eva. She told her again that this was to be her permanent home, and, in a few months' time, when she left school, she would be able to get a job.

"I didn't want to go back to Germany. I wanted to stay here in Wales, but I wish I could see Mama and Papa, and Iwan again." She asked, "Did the Germans kill them?"

"Iwan died of typhoid in a labour camp. It was the Nazis who killed your Mama and Papa, they killed millions of other people too."

"Mama and Papa were German, so why would they want to kill them?"

"It's a very complicated thing, Eva; no one fully understands, but over the next few days we'll try to explain it to you as best we can."

Nancy caught sight of Glynn with one of the dogs. Tom wouldn't be far away. "Look, there's Glynn, he'll be wanting to know how you are, shall we tell him you're going to be all right?"

"Yes," said Eva. Then she said, "I wish I wasn't German; I wish I was the same as everyone else here."

"You will be soon, because you're going to be a British citizen."

"I will? When?" asked Eva.

"As soon as it's official; we're going to complete the documents tonight and post them tomorrow morning."

Tom joined Glynn when he saw Nancy and Eva approaching, "All right?" Tom asked Eva; she nodded bravely.

"That's the ticket!" declared Glynn, feeling slightly awkward.

"Are you coming back for something to eat now?" Nancy asked them.

"Might as well; we had an early breakfast," replied Tom, taking Eva's arm and tucking it though his. Glynn took her other one, and they strolled back to the house arm in arm. Nancy watched her three young people getting on so well together. *We have a daughter, a lovely teenage daughter*, she thought. She looked up at the clouds and thought of Frieda Aarons and the cruel hand she'd been dealt; tears sprang into her eyes. In her mind, she spoke to Frieda. "We'll look after her. She'll have a good life, I promise you."

Barbara called at the farm to see Eva on her way home from school. They went up to her room and sat on the bed.

"Miss Hughes told us what happened to your family. I knew already, because Mam told me last night. I'm glad you're not going back to Germany."

"So am I," said Eva. "Auntie Nan said I can start to think about a job, now that I'm staying here."

"Are you going to be adopted?" asked Barbara, "You're an orphan now, aren't you?"

"I shouldn't think so; aren't I too old to be adopted?"

"I don't know, but Mr. and Mrs. Morgan are your Mam and Dad now, aren't they?"

"I always think of them as my parents, I don't remember my real ones; I can't remember what they looked like or anything," said Eva sadly. "I always thought they would come for me, but now I know they won't."

The girls chatted until it was time for Barbara to leave. "Are you going to school tomorrow?" she asked.

"No, I'm going to stay here with Auntie Nan, she wants me with her because she's going to explain some things about the war; I'll call round on Saturday afternoon if you like."

"See you on Saturday, then," Barbara said as she left.

Nancy kept Eva off school for the rest of the week, and tried to explain her understanding of the war's prejudice and cruelty; that good overcame evil, and now everyone must look to the future.

On Friday of that week, the whole family had the day off and went to Swansea, because Stan wanted to see what the town was like now. There had been a lot of serious damage during the bombing raids, and huge areas of the town centre had been destroyed; the flames from burning buildings had been seen from as far away as the North Devon Coast. There were many bomb sites, although life was gradually getting back to normal.

Dai paid Eva a visit on Saturday morning, and gave her the small bunch of wild flowers he'd picked from the hedgerow in the lane; she was pleased to see him, and he stayed with her for most of the morning.

At bedtime, Nancy went into Eva's room. Eva spoke when she kissed her good night. "Auntie Nan?"

"Yes, what is it?" asked Nancy.

"I've been wondering: is it all right if I call you Mam?"

Nancy almost wept. "Oh, child, of course it is." She sat on the bed and held Eva's hand. "And what about Uncle Stan, would you like to call him Dad?"

"Yes, I would," replied Eva.

"Mam and Dad it is then," said Nancy. She kissed Eva good night and went downstairs. Stan looked up from his paper when she entered the room. Her eyes glistened. "You'll never guess…"

Chapter Seven
June 1948

The time came for Eva's year to leave school; she said a tearful goodbye to the teachers, and walked home with Barbara for the last time. There was to be no long summer holiday, because they were starting work on the following Monday.

Barbara had a job in the woollen mill; she was going to learn all the processes, beginning with carding and spinning. Once she mastered that, she would be taught to dye the wool and weave it into cloth.

Dai had no option other than to work in the mine. His dictatorial father told him that was where he was going to work, and gave him no choice in the matter.

Eva got her wish, because demand for transport was still increasing and outstripping the haulier's resources; the two pre-war lorries had been replaced with three brand new ones and more drivers were recruited. The old office clerk was struggling and unable to cope, so the director decided to recruit a school leaver, and gave the job to Eva.

Stan and Nancy gave her a secondhand typewriter for Christmas; she had been teaching herself to type since, and was looking forward to being competent enough to use the one in the office.

"You're getting quite good at typing," said Nancy. "Why not practice with the farm's accounts? We could do them in parallel;

if yours look better than my handwritten ones, we'll use yours instead."

"I'd like that; do you think I might have a table in my room so I can do my typing in there?"

"Good thinking," replied Nancy, pleased that she wasn't going to be listening to the clatter of the typewriter in the kitchen. "Are you excited about starting work?"

"Can't wait!"

Eva's first day was daunting, and she felt in the way; the office clerk was irritable and didn't seem able to find time to show her anything. She filed documents in the cabinet, and did jobs the clerk didn't want to do. At the end of the day, she put on her coat and stout shoes for the long walk home. She noticed Kathleen. She was waiting for her boyfriend, Mick. "Eva! How was your first day?"

"All right, but I'll feel better when I know what to do without being told," she replied.

Kathleen noticed she was prepared for the walk home. "Are you going to be walking to work every day?"

Eva nodded.

"Can you ride a bike?" Kathleen asked her.

"No, I've never been on one."

"If you're willing to learn, I have an old one I don't use any more; you can have it if you like. It needs a lot of work, but I'm sure Glynn or Tom can fix it for you."

"I'd love a bike; yes, please! Shall I ask one of them to collect it?"

"Yes, any time. I'll get it ready—if I'm not there when he comes, someone will be."

Tom went to Kathleen's house to collect the bicycle that evening; she heard a truck stop outside. When she opened the front door, she saw Tom Morgan lowering the tailgate.

"Go round the back through the entry, it's in the yard," she said, and went through the house to open the gate for him. "Here it is; I've given it a wipe to get the dust off." The bike was leaning against the wall, and was a comical sight. "It needs a bit of work before she can use it," Kathleen said helpfully.

"You can say that again!" laughed Tom, looking at the wreck before him. "How old is it?"

"I've had it since I was twelve; it was ancient then. I reckon it must be at least twenty years old."

"That's nothing for a Raleigh; last a lifetime, this will," he said, pulling it away from the wall for a better appraisal. "I'll get the rust off and paint the frame. We've got some green and black paint we use for the farm machinery; she can choose which colour she wants. It only needs new tyres and a saddle, by the look of it; I reckon she'll be using it next week."

He wheeled it down the entry, saying, "She hasn't ridden a bike before. The village is getting quite busy these days; I hope she's got some road sense."

"I can teach her," said Kathleen. "She can practice on my other bike after work; once she's got her balance she'll soon get the hang of what she's meant to do in traffic."

"She'll like that; shall I bring her round for an hour tomorrow evening? I'll come back and collect her when you've shown her what to do." Tom put the bike on to the back of the truck, shut the tailgate, and got into the cab. "See you tomorrow?"

"Yes, see you tomorrow," she replied.

"Is that it?" said Glynn, looking at the rusty old heap before him. "You'd better make a start tonight if you expect her to be using it for work on Monday."

"I know; you just wait and see, it'll look like new by the time I've finished with it. I'm going to strip it right down and repaint it; all it'll need is a new saddle and tyres."

"Where will you get the tyres from? Have you thought about asking the haulier? He should be able to get them at a good price for you," suggested Glynn.

"Good idea. I'll give Eva a lift tomorrow morning and ask him." Tom took Eva to work, and then went to look for Mick; he found him in the yard, and asked him. Mick nodded, "Yes, I can get them for you. What size do you need, twenty-six inches? I've got an order with the supplier at the moment; I'll give them a ring and add yours to it."

"Thanks. Will you let Eva know when they've arrived?"

"Yes, I'll tell her."

"We'll go for a drink when I collect them; it's on me." Tom called at the hardware shop on his way home, and bought a new saddle, a lamp and a puncture repair kit.

Tom took Eva for her cycling lesson. "Stay if you like, you don't have to leave," said Kathleen. He decided to stay; they held the bike steady, while Eva found her balance; gradually she grew confident and they were able to let go. How she loved the wind on her face and in her hair on that fine summer's evening! It was exhilarating. She pedalled back up the street to where they were waiting. "Oh, I did enjoy that," she said, reluctantly getting off the bike.

"So we see; your face is all rosy!" Kathleen exclaimed.

"We'd better get going; we've been here over two hours. I'll bring her again tomorrow if you're free; we won't stay as long next time," Tom said apologetically.

Next evening, Kathleen instructed Eva how she should ride her bike in traffic. "She could do with the Highway Code," she said.

"We've got one somewhere; Dad bought it when we were learning to drive. Mam will know where it is."

"Eva, would you like another practice? You can stay another half an hour, can't you, Tom?"

He nodded. "Let's walk to the park while we wait for her. I think Mick will get the new tyres tomorrow. If he does, I'll meet him in the Collier's Arms and he can give them to me there."

"You won't be coming tomorrow, then?" Kathleen asked, disappointed.

"No, she's quite competent isn't she?" he replied, missing the nuance in Kathleen's question.

"Unless you feel a bit more practice…" she said, hopefully. He picked it up this time; why not? He had enjoyed the last two evenings.

It was busy in the pub on Friday; Mick and Tom waited their turn. "Two pints of mild, please." Tom paid for the drinks and handed one to Mick; they drank their beer at the bar, and ordered another.

"How's the bike coming on?" asked Mick.

"It's still in pieces at the moment; it needs one more coat of paint, but she'll be able to use it for work on Monday. It's a good job it's a lady's bike, or I'd be wanting to keep it for myself."

"Watch Kath doesn't want it back, then," laughed Mick.

Tom paused a moment and asked, "Will you and Kath be getting married any time soon, do you think?"

"I don't think so, I don't really want to be married, and she never mentions it; I don't think she's bothered either."

After another pint, they left the pub, and Tom gave him the money for the tyres. "Thanks a lot, Mick, I'll see you around."

"See you mate, we'll have another pint sometime."

"Well, would you look at this!" declared Glynn, as Tom wheeled the smart black bicycle into the kitchen.

"You've made a good job of that, son," said Stan. "It looks brand new."

"Where's Eva?" Tom asked.

"She's gone to the shops with Mam; they'll be back soon."

Nancy and Eva were in the village, buying provisions for the weekend; they called at the bakery, because Nancy wanted to thank Kath for the bike. "Come round for tea one day next week; what about Tuesday?"

"I'd like that, but if it's no bother, Wednesday would be better, because it's my half day off, and it won't be such a rush."

"Wednesday's fine, we usually eat at around six o'clock; do come earlier if you can," replied Nancy.

Eva drew breath when she saw the bike; it looked splendid. The smell of new tyres and shiny black paint made it as though it had just left the factory; she was thrilled, and wanted to ride it immediately.

"Have something to eat first; then you may go," said Nancy.

Eva rose early for work on Monday morning. "She looks so grown up, doesn't she? Cycling off to work like that," Nancy remarked to Stan, as they watched her pedal down the lane.

Kath arrived at five o'clock on Wednesday afternoon; she had been looking forward to going to the Morgans, and had spent a long time getting ready. She had visited the farm a few years ago, when Eva first started school, but she hadn't been since. She liked it there; she liked the views across the cwm to the hills, and she liked the house with its huge welcoming kitchen. She especially liked to see the sheep grazing, and to watch the hens as they scratched the earth, searching for insects.

Kath lived with her parents and brothers in a terraced house on one of the village's narrow streets. It had a backyard which was accessed through an entry shared with next door. The only animals she ever had any contact with were their terrier dog and budgerigar.

She admired her old bicycle, which now looked better than her present one; she watched Eva demonstrate her shorthand and typing skills, and simply enjoyed just being there. Nancy noticed that Tom had made more effort than usual with his appearance; she watched him showing off at the tea table, and thought, *He's trying to make an impression, and succeeding, by the look of things.*

Nancy liked Kathleen; she and her best friend Mabel had been very kind to Eva when she had first arrived in Wales; they used to take her, and Barbara sometimes, for a walk to the swings in the park. She mused as she watched her now with Tom. *She'd be a good match for him, and a nice addition to the family.*

After tea, Nancy heard Tom ask Kath if she would like to look around the farm, and perhaps walk down the field to the ford. *Oh dear,* she thought, *the girl's got her best clothes on.* She intervened, "It's a pity to get your shoes muddy; I'm sure I could find you a pair of wellingtons if you don't mind wearing them, and I have a wind-cheater you could borrow."

Kath accepted Nancy's offer, and went with Tom to see the farm and the lowland. When Nancy and Eva were washing the dishes, Eva gave Nancy a playful nudge and a knowing look, they both burst out laughing at the thought of Tom courting.

Kath and Tom became inseparable. Kath was happiest when she was helping Tom and Nancy with the animals, and every day after work she cycled to the farm to be with them.

"We hardly ever see our girl these days," said her father, arriving home from work and finding his daughter absent again.

"Oh, she's all right," replied her mother. "She's at Tom's. I wouldn't be at all surprised if there's a wedding next year; I think we'd better start saving."

"He's a nice lad, that Tom, she could do a lot worse. Good family, the Morgans; not many would be prepared to take in a child from another country." Trying to think back, he asked, "They lost one, didn't they?"

"Yes, they did, a baby girl. She died when Glynn was about eighteen months old; they never fully recovered, but when Tom was born I think they came to terms."

At the beginning of December, Tom was in the truck with Stan on their way home from the market.

"Dad, I'm going to ask Kath to marry me; I want us to get engaged at Christmas."

"Have you spoken to her father?"

"No."

"Well, you should. I know she's over twenty-one, but it's only common courtesy, you know."

"What do you think, Dad? Will Mam be pleased?" asked Tom, wanting their approval.

"I think you've made an excellent choice; we both like Kath, and we think she'll make you a good wife."

Tom grinned, "I'll tell Mam as soon as we get home."

Nancy was delighted. "A Christmas engagement, how lovely! I'm thrilled for you, son; shall we have a celebration?" Of course, her feelings were somewhat mixed. Tom was her baby, after all; imagining him married with a family of his own was quite difficult— but who better than Kath?

"I haven't asked her yet."

"Well, you'd better get on with it, then, and don't forget you'll need to buy a ring."

Tom laughed, "Knowing her, she'll want to choose it herself. We're going Christmas shopping in Swansea soon, she can choose it then."

Kath was on her way to the farm; it was a cold dark evening and her bicycle lamp cast a bouncy glow on the lane as she pedalled faster to get into the warm. Tom was waiting for her and started to walk up the lane; he saw the bike's lamp flickering in the distance and he quickened his pace. When they met, he gave her a lingering kiss, "Get up on the seat and I'll give you a croggy." Tom straddled the bike and pedalled while Kath clung to him, trying to keep her balance on the bumpy lane.

"Hello Kath, bitter out there isn't it?" said Nancy, "The fire's lit in the front room, warm yourself in there."

Tom looked at his mother quizzically. "Go on, then," she whispered, indicating he was meant to go in there too.

After a short while, the excited couple returned to the kitchen, and Kath exclaimed, "We're getting married!"

"Oh my goodness," said Nancy, "I'm very pleased. And there's going to be another Mrs. Morgan!"

"Congratulations," said Stan. "We couldn't be happier."

"Seems I'm getting another sister! Well done, Tom, congratulations!" added Glynn.

Eva was full of joy; her beloved Kath was going to be her sister-in-law. "Am I going to be a bridesmaid?"

"Of course you are, you're my first choice," laughed Kath, giving her a hug.

"We'd better go and tell your family now," said Tom. "Is it all right if I take the truck, Dad?"

"Help yourself; you know where the keys are. Take your back door key as well, in case you're late back," replied Stan. Tom put the bike on to the back of the truck, and drove to Kath's house to tell her parents the happy news.

"It's thrilled we are – welcome to the family, son!" said her delighted father.

Chapter Eight

When Dai left school, he was one of three boys starting work at the colliery; most of the other boys leaving that term had apprenticeships in Port Talbot, either at the foundry or the Railway and Docks Company. Those professions offered good job prospects, unlike the declining coal industry.

During the past nine years, Head Mistress Hughes had regarded Dai as one of her stars; he was a bright lad throughout his school days and she felt frustrated, because he should have gone to the grammar school. She had spoken to his father, but he would have none of it; he wouldn't even consider letting him go into the steel industry. She didn't understand the man at all, surely anyone who had worked in a coal mine since childhood would want his son to do something else.

Being a collier meant that Dai would be exempt from National Service. However, Miss Hughes saw an opportunity, and she was going to give him some advice. "Dai, come to my office, I want to speak to you."

She closed the door and asked, "If you were able, what would you choose for your occupation?"

Dai hadn't thought about it, because Dad had given him no choice; he was expected to be a collier, like all the other men in the family. "I don't know, Miss; my mates are going to Port Talbot. I think I would like to work down there."

She thought a moment and said, "Do what your father wants for now, and learn all you can at the colliery. When you're eighteen, you'll be old enough for National Service, and I urge you to think about joining, because I'm certain you'll benefit from the experience. You'll meet people from all walks of life and it will open opportunities for you; will you at least consider it, when the time comes?"

"Yes, Miss, I will. Thank you, Miss."

"Off you go, then. Good Luck!"

"Thank you, Miss," he said, and left her office.

"Come on, Davey, lad, you don't want to be late on your first day," Gil Jenkins said, as he woke his youngest son at the crack of dawn. Dai was starting work as an apprentice at the colliery. He had not been ready to leave school; he knew that Miss Hughes had spoken to Dad about allowing him to stay on at school a bit longer, but Dad had refused to.

Money was tight in the Jenkins's household, because most of the wage earners had left home. Dai's two elder brothers were married, with families of their own to support. The last brother living at home was Sam; he was engaged to one of the blacksmith's daughters, and was going to live at the smithy after he married.

Another brother had been killed in France during the war. Martin had been a stretcher bearer taking an injured soldier to a field hospital, when he was hit by the shell that killed him. He could have continued working in the mine, but he wanted to get away from Manddiogel and see the world. He joined the army and went to France; five months later he was dead.

Mam had saved his old clothes and boots for Dai; he was going to wear those boots today. They were still too big, so she stuffed some old cloth into them, to make a better fit.

Mary was unmarried and almost thirty; she had left home years ago, and lived above her tailoring shop in the village; Ethel was nineteen and still lived at home. She had left school unable to read or write, and had never been able to find suitable work. There were some truly awful jobs for women at the pit, and at other premises around the village—usually dealing with waste, or cleaning up the mess in slaughter houses. Gil and Em were not prepared to have their daughter do that sort of work for a pittance, so she stayed at home and helped with the housework.

"Come on short-shanks, let's get you started," said the foreman. "You'll make a miner just like your dad; you'll soon get some muscles on those bones once you start shifting that coal."

The foreman gave Dai a metal disk with a number stamped on it and said, "Take this check to the lamp-man over there, and he'll give you a lamp with the same number on it; this check is very important because it tells the boss who's underground. Your life will depend on this in the event of an accident. If you're in trouble down there, and your check is hanging on that board, someone will come to your aid."

The lamp-man took the check from Dai; he removed lamp number 847 from its hook and gave it to him. "This is your lamp, number 847, the same number as your check. Bring your lamp back here when you've finished your shift and the check will be returned to you. Take it home and keep it safe, make sure you bring it with you every time. You'll need it to get your wages as well; best to wear it around your neck so you don't lose it."

Dai put his helmet on and fixed its battery on to his belt; the foreman did the same with his. They joined the queue at the shaft, and waited for the lift to arrive at the surface. The gate was pulled open, and it filled with men; and when it closed, they went down into the gloom. Dai had never felt such fear. The lift came to an abrupt halt at the bottom of the shaft, after what seemed an age.

He was now in a cavernous space; some of the tunnels running off were over a mile long.

There were unfamiliar noises: he could hear ponies, and the metallic rattle of wheels on rails, water dripping from the roof splashed into puddles. The supporting timbers were creaking, and the sound of machinery and men echoed in the tunnels.

The air was thick; he could smell sweaty bodies in filthy clothes, the damp straw in the ponies' stalls, and the coal dust, waiting to be breathed and do its worst.

Dai started as a sorter-boy, separating ore from gangue; sometimes he was a truck pusher, working with the ponies. There were tests to pass before he moved to the next stage of his apprenticeship; he learned quickly and gained the practical experience needed for the hewer exam when he was twenty.

The National Coal Board took ownership of the mine at the beginning of the year; improvements were quickly made, because the mines in this region were antiquated and dangerous. This mine was one of the larger ones, and the first to get better lighting, gas detection, and cutting equipment.

It was the introduction of machinery that caught Dai's interest; he enjoyed tinkering with it during his snap break. He oiled cogs and bearings, sharpened blades, and generally kept it clean and in good order. However, he was employed as a miner, not a mechanic, and it was he who was sent into the narrowest seams because he was the smallest. He crawled on all fours, with the roof of the tunnel just inches above him; sometimes it took over an hour to get to the face. It was hot in the narrow seams, and he usually worked in only his underpants. By the end of the shift he could hardly stand, because his legs were so painful after being cramped for so long.

There were several songs and poems miners used to boost morale. He liked this one best because it reminded him of Granny; she used to sing it to him when he was a little boy:

> *I am a little collier and working underground*
> *The rope will never break when I go up and down*
> *It's bread when I'm hungry*
> *And beer when I'm dry*
> *It's bed when I'm tired*
> *And heaven when I die*

It seemed to Dai that this was his lot; he could see no way of getting off this tread-mill. He saw very little of his friends, because either he was at work, or they were. Sometimes he caught a glimpse of Eva laughing with a group of friends as they walked down the street; she always looked tidy and well groomed. He felt like a tramp in comparison. There was always a friendly wave if she saw him, then something would grab her attention, and she was gone.

One morning, three years later, he saw Miss Hughes coming out of the Post Office; she asked him how he was getting on, he told her truthfully.

"You know, Dai, there's no reason why work should take over your entire life, you get some spare time surely," she considered a moment. "Do you read books?"

"No, we don't have any in the house."

"Have you not seen the mobile library? It comes to the village every Thursday morning, there's hundreds of books; you pick the ones you want to borrow, return them within three weeks, and choose some more."

He brightened. "I didn't know about the library. Does it have educational books as well, I can never remember if they're called fiction, or non-fiction?"

"They do. The best way to remember the difference is: fiction is short for fictitious, meaning created by the imagination, or false. Non-fiction is fact and reality—encyclopaedias, history, and geography books are non-fiction," she explained.

"I've got a morning shift this Thursday. The week after, I think I'm on afternoons; do you know what time it comes?" he asked.

"It arrives outside the village hall at eleven o'clock, it stays for about an hour, and then goes to the other villages. It parks in some of the lanes along the way for about fifteen minutes, so that those people living remotely can use it as well."

"Thank you, Miss Hughes; I'll definitely start to use it."

"I hope you do; I might see you there, I use it too."

On Thursday the following week, Dai had the whole morning off, because he wasn't due at work until the afternoon. He walked to the village, and waited for the library to arrive. He joined the short queue and waited his turn; he enrolled and entered another world. All the story books were on the left, and all the non-fiction ones were grouped by subject on the right.

"How many books did you say I could borrow at a time?" he asked, spoilt for choice.

"Three," was the reply. *Oh dear,* he thought. *I don't know where to start, there are so many.* He chose a geography book, a volume of Encyclopaedia Britannica, and a model engineering book; the librarian stamped the due to return date in the front of the books and removed the tickets from each one.

"Hello there," said a familiar voice. "Which ones have you chosen?" It was Reverend Pritchard. Dai showed him his choice.

"Serious stuff here, no stories then? Try a novel sometime, something by Nevil Shute or Evelyn Waugh, I think you'd enjoy a spot of fiction, it'll take you to another place; it can be just as educational, you know."

"I will. Thank you." Dai couldn't wait to get home and look at the books; he remembered Miss Hughes's words on the day he left school, and what she had said to him recently about using his time wisely. He decided to learn all he could, and when he was eighteen, he was going speak to his father about joining the army.

Mary Jenkins halted the treadle on her machine and looked out of the window; she saw a couple of youths chatting in the street. *There's our Dai,* she thought, and tapped on the window. Dai looked across and waved; a few moments later he walked into her workshop.

"Hello Mary, busy?"

"As always," she replied, lighting the gas under the kettle. "I can barely cope; people moving into the new council houses want curtains making, and I've got two wedding dresses and seven bridesmaids' dresses to make before July."

She passed him his tea and regarded him critically; he looked grimy and sallow. She wondered: *Does this boy ever see daylight? He wouldn't see much, because during the winter it would be dark when he started his shift and dark when he finished; if he was on nights, he'd be asleep during the day.* His clothes were shabby and worn; she thought she recognised them as Martin's old things.

"Have you any other trousers, Dai, because if you have, I'd chuck those out they're threadbare."

"I've only got my pit ones."

"Time you bought some new ones then."

"I haven't any money."

"What do you mean you haven't any money, you're getting paid aren't you?"

"I have to give it all to Dad; sometimes he gives me pocket money."

"Pocket money, at your age!" Mary was incensed. "Are you telling me you're not paying board yet?"

"Yes, I only get pocket money."

"The mean old devil! If you're not paying board, he should buy you some clothes; what do you wear when you meet your friends?"

"I don't go out much, my mates tend to stay down at Port Talbot after work and go out from there; I wouldn't want to go to the pub, because Dad would be there with his cronies."

"What about Eva, why don't you ask her to go out with you?" *He'll have to smarten himself, and he's no money to take a girl on a date, so that's not likely to happen,* she thought sadly.

"I haven't seen much of Eva since we left school, and anyway the farm lads like her; she wouldn't want me, because they're taller and better looking than I am."

"Nonsense!" declared Mary. "Look at the muscles on you, you've got a handsome face, you'd be even more handsome if you got the coal muck out of your pores and tidied yourself. Some of the farm lads might be tall and healthy looking, but you're good looking too, and fun to be with, or you were; make the most of what you've got!"

Mary looked at her youngest brother, he seemed so depressed and careworn these days, he had been such a happy child with his school friends and his little girlfriend, Eva. Mary reckoned he had loved her from the moment he set eyes on her, from that day she had arrived at school, that frightened infant from Germany who couldn't speak a word of English. Those two had walked miles with Rusty, along the cwm and up and over the hills. *I wonder what they talked about in those carefree days*, she mused.

Remembering Miss Hughes's advice to Dai, she asked, "Have any of your friends been called up for National Service yet?"

"No, but I don't think it'll be long before they are."

"And what about you, are you going to join?" Mary asked, imagining Dad's reaction.

"I was going to speak to Dad, but I know he won't allow it, because he can't afford for me to go."

"Funny how he always manages to find the money for his beer and fags though." She had the measure of their dad. Of course he hadn't let Dai stay on at school or go to the steelworks; he had plans for his youngest, for sure. He intended him to work at the pit, marry a local girl and bring her to live with them. He would take over the rent book, and Mam and Dad would have a roof over their heads and someone to care for them, for life, the crafty selfish old sod.

"Would you like join the National Service?" Mary asked.

Dai nodded.

"Well, let's find out about it."

They contacted the Government, and within a few months Dai received his call-up papers. He had a date and place to report for duty; all that remained now was to tell Mam and Dad. Mary advised him to say nothing until he had been accepted and knew when and where he was going; she knew he would have difficulty telling them, so she offered to go with him and give him some support.

"Look Dad, our Dai ought to be doing something else, he'll have an opportunity to learn a skill in the army, something he can use to get a more suitable job when he's finished his time there. It's dangerous in the mines, I know they're safer now the NCB own them, but there's still far too many accidents."

Mary looked at her father and scrutinised him; she supposed he must have looked presentable once, a long time ago, although she didn't remember him looking any differently, just a bit younger.

He was stockily built, with small blue scars on his hands and face, the result of new skin growing over coal dust not removed from cuts and grazes properly. The first and second fingers on his right hand were stained with nicotine, and some of his teeth were missing; those remaining were long, loose and nicotine stained. He had worked at the same pit all his life. A quiet man, and incredibly selfish, he gave Mam scant housekeeping money and spent the rest of his wages on beer and tobacco.

"We need him here with us; he'll have a good job at the pit when he's qualified. He's not taken the hewer exam yet, why should he join the army?" Gil said, knowing perfectly well.

"I'm not going over it again, Dad; he wants to go and he's going." Mary was getting frustrated. "If it's the money that's bothering you, he can send you some of his pay, and I'll help out if you get short. Don't worry about Ethel, she can move in with me; I've plenty of jobs she can do in the workshop."

Mary won the argument. Gil and Em were getting on in years now, and they were stuck in their old ways; she decided it was time to take charge. Her thinking was broad, and her judgement sound. Dai needed someone to envisage his future and to help him have a better life. Who would want this bright youngster to end up like the worn-out old man sitting in front of them? As usual, Mam said nothing; she would go along with Dad, no matter what she thought.

Gil reluctantly agreed; Mary gave him no choice. Ethel joined them and they discussed the situation further. She was going to live and work with Mary, instead of in that gloomy old pit house with Mam and Dad and their miserable old-fashioned ways, and Dai was joining the army.

He walked his sister home. "Thank you, Mary, I couldn't have done that."

"You're still very young. I was like you once, leaving home was hard for me too; but I was desperate to go and it was the best thing I did." She gave him a quick hug, and said good night.

Dai returned home to a different atmosphere. His father was deflated, because he realised that his youngest was grown and ready to find his own place in the world, a world much larger than his. He couldn't understand why young people weren't content with things as they were; why did they want to keep changing things?

Chapter Nine
1952

Barbara's shift was finished, and she was making her way home down the lane; she thought she recognised the soldier getting out of a lorry at the crossroads, and she quickened her pace.

"Hello Dai, home for a spot of leave?"

"Yes, until Monday; I thought I'd better come home this time because Dad's not too good. I don't know when I'll be back, because I'm being posted abroad. How are you?"

"I'm well, thanks."

"And everyone else?"

"I take it you mean Eva?"

"Yes, how is she?"

"She's fine."

"What's she doing? Is she courting?"

"She's not short of dates, but there's no one special; she seems more interested in her job, she does all the typing and book keeping now. They've set up a new depot and head office in Cardiff; she can do shorthand, so I wouldn't be at all surprised if they offered her a secretarial job down there."

"Would she go, do you think?"

"I don't think so," said Barbara. "I can't see her leaving Manddiogel."

They walked together until they reached the old foot path leading to Felin Fach. "Have you any plans for tomorrow evening

Dai? There's always a dance at the Miners' Welfare on Saturdays. Eva and I go every week."

"I've nothing planned; what time does it start?"

"About half past seven; perhaps we'll see you there. I hope things aren't too bad at home."

Dai arrived at the old pit cottage and dropped his kit-bag on the scullery floor; it was eerily quiet. He went upstairs. There was no one there, so he went back downstairs and into the tiny sitting room, where he found his desperately sick father lying in an ancient single bed.

"Hello Dad, where's Mam?"

Gil struggled to tell him that she was on her way back from the village with his prescription. Dai looked at his father; there was nothing left of him. He was just a tiny being, lost among the bedclothes. "Can I get you something? I'm going to put the kettle on." Gil declined by closing his eyes.

While he was in the scullery he heard the latch click as the back door opened. "Dai," said his weary mother, giving him a quick peck on the cheek. "It's good to see you, son; how long are you here for?"

"Until Monday. Things not too good, I see."

"No, it's bad; he has a nasty cough and can't get his breath. Our Sam and someone from the smithy brought one of the beds downstairs, and put it in there to save my legs. Ethel comes after work to help me with him and stays the night. You won't get any sleep here; if I were you I'd ask our Mary if you can sleep in Ethel's bed, she doesn't need it at the moment. Are you hungry?"

He was starving, but could see his mother was in no fit state to cook him a meal. "I'll go and see Mary and ask if I can stay with her; I'll bring us some fish and chips back."

Ethel was almost ready to leave the workshop and go to Mam's for the night. She had been doing this for the past few weeks, and the strain was showing. Mary let her have a sleep in the afternoons, knowing she'd get very little during the night. Both women were happy to see their youngest brother again. He looked so much better since he had joined the army; the pallor of his face had been replaced with a healthy out-of-doors glow. It was agreed that he should use Ethel's room. Mary was delighted to have him there, and was looking forward to hearing about his army life.

Dai helped Ethel with her coat, and picked up her bag of shopping. "We're going to get some fish and chips on the way back; do you want some, Mary?"

"Yes, I'll come with you, but I'll bring mine back here. I'll just be a tick," she replied, while fetching her coat and purse.

When Ethel and Dai arrived at the cottage, Em had the oven on, ready to reheat the fish and chips, and was making a pot of tea. Ethel took Gil a half-filled mug and a small portion of Mam's fish; he managed a few sips of tea, but couldn't eat anything, so she gave him his medicine instead.

"What's in that?" asked Dai, when she returned with the medicine bottle.

"It's a mixture of morphine and some other stuff, it settles him when he becomes agitated."

By the time they had eaten it was almost seven o'clock. Dai picked up his kit-bag and said he would see them in the morning. When he arrived at Mary's flat, he put his things in Ethel's room and joined Mary in the lounge; they sat together on the settee and she told him her plans.

"When Dad's gone, Mam is coming to live with us."

"Will she sleep with Ethel?" he asked, considering the limited space.

"No, I'm going to buy a house; there's a nice three bedroomed semi come up for sale, about half a mile down the main road. I've enough saved for a deposit, and the bank says it will lend me the rest. My business is doing really well, so I'm going to convert this room into a sewing room, and turn downstairs into a shop, selling fabrics and ready-made things. Ethel's had a go on the machine, and she's quite good; with practice, I think she'll be very good. I've cut out and tacked simple things like cushions and curtains and she's machined them for me. She takes her time, but she'll get quicker. When Mam no longer needs her, she'll have a full-time job as the machinist. There'll be plenty for Mam to do here, keeping it clean and tidy, and there'll be the house and garden to see to as well. She's looking forward to it; she said when she gets her pension, she'll put that into the pot as well."

"Sounds as though you've got it all planned," said Dai. He was pleased for her; it would be nice to see her hard work rewarded.

"I think we'll see a big change in Mam once she's out of that miserable marriage. Now tell me: what have you been up to while you've been away, and where are you being posted?" Dai told her about his engineering course in England, and how much he was looking forward to going to Suez.

"Have you stayed in touch with Eva?"

"Sort of; she writes to me sometimes."

"You probably know that Tom Morgan married Kathleen, and there's a second baby on the way. The farmhouse has been extended, it's got a bathroom now, and there's plans to build a bothy on the side for Glynn so he'll have a place of his own.

Apparently Mr. and Mrs. Morgan senior are having a bungalow built for themselves next door because the house is getting a bit crowded."

People were arriving at the dance; Dai was there already, chatting with a group of old friends at the bar. When Barbara and Eva had finished tidying themselves after being wind-blown, they made their way to the dance floor. "See who's over there?" said Barbara, nudging Eva.

"Where?"

"Over there, look, by the bar." She pointed out Dai in the group of young men shrouded in cigarette smoke. "Shall we join them?"

"No need; they're coming over," replied Eva.

The men joined the girls, and Dai asked Eva if she would like to dance; at the end of the evening he asked if he could walk her home, and was disappointed when she said Glynn was coming in the car to collect her.

On Sunday, Dai made an impromptu visit to the farm, hoping to find Eva there. Nancy opened the door and looked with pleasant surprise at the fellow standing before her; the little boy who'd stood on this doorstep countless times before was now a man. *How quickly the years have passed*, she thought sadly.

"Come in, lad," she said, opening the door wide. "Eva's in the small barn with Tom's son, Paul; she's showing him the puppies that were born yesterday. Go and find her; you know where it is."

Eva and Paul were watching the little black and white puppies crawling over each other. She was explaining that the one with the white patch over his eye was the alpha puppy; he was slightly heavier than the others, and instinctively went to the teat closest to his mother's back leg, to prevent his siblings muscling in from the side.

"There's clever!" remarked Dai.

Eva was pleased to see her old friend again. "Hello, Dai. I'm showing this little one our new arrivals; aren't they cute? I'm observing them while they're in the nest, because we're going to keep two and sell the rest. These are descended from Meg, so they should fetch a good price." Getting up off her knees and taking hold of Paul's hand, she asked, "Fancy a walk? We could take Paul to the park."

The little boy squealed with joy as Dai pushed him higher and higher in the baby swing; Eva took him down the slide and on the roundabout. "Are you going to stay for tea?" she asked on their way back to the farm.

"I can't; I'd like to, but I must see Dad before I go back to barracks, and Mary's cooking something for me later. I'd better get off, I've got a very early start in the morning," he said with regret. "Write to me while I'm abroad, here's the address." He handed his overseas address to Eva, which she put safely in her handbag.

Dai gently patted his father's arm when he said goodbye, knowing this was going to be the last time he would see him. He spent a sad, yet pleasant evening with Mary, and caught the first bus out of the village the following morning; three days later, he was on his way to Suez with the Royal Engineers.

Gil Jenkins died in the early hours of the morning with Em and Ethel by his bedside; the relief his wife and daughter felt was immeasurable. They had nursed him for a very long time hoping peace would come soon, and now, at last, it had.

Not long after the funeral, Mary got the keys to her new house. It was attractive, with bay windows, a front porch and three bedrooms; the two front ones had views across the main road to the distant hills. The third bedroom overlooked the back garden and some waste ground where a footpath ran alongside a cluster of allotments. Next to that bedroom was a small bathroom and a separate toilet. Downstairs, there was a kitchen with a pantry, a pleasant sitting room with French doors giving access to the back garden, and the bay-windowed front room where she was going to put the dining table.

Mary and Ethel moved in first; they cleared the cottage of Gil's old things, sorted out Em's meagre belongings, most of which she threw out, and handed the cottage back to the Coal Board.

Mary converted her old workroom on the ground floor into a shop selling ready-made soft furnishings, material and threads; the two former bedrooms upstairs became the sewing room and a stockroom. She was pleased with her achievement, everything had fallen into place; Ethel became the full time machinist, and Mam was responsible for keeping the house and workshop clean and tidy. Both were much happier, and no longer looked scrawny and anxious.

***

When Dai returned from Suez, his National Service was over; he had acquired the skills he needed, and was feeling confident about his future. He intended to get an engineering job in Leicestershire and move there, with Eva as his wife. He was back in Wales and staying at Mary's house. He told his mother and sisters the plan. "I can't see Eva moving to England, can you?" said Em, looking at Mary doubtfully.

"No, I'm afraid I can't; have you asked her yet, Dai?"

"I almost mentioned it in a letter, but I thought I'd wait and talk to her about it."

Dai and Eva went to the pub that evening and discussed their future at length. Dai said that he wanted to move to what he saw as a brighter future for them both, while Eva replied that she wanted to stay in the village where she felt secure.

"I can't leave here, Dai, I'm sorry, really I can't. This is the only place I've ever felt safe; all our friends are here. Why go all that way to a place we don't know? It doesn't make any sense."

"But it does Eva, there's a lot of good jobs there for both of us; it's a nice area, right in the heart of England. We'll soon make new friends."

"What's wrong with here? There's plenty of engineering jobs down at the port, and there's jobs on the surface of the collieries."

"I want something new; I've seen places and done things I never thought I would. I can't face coming back here," he replied with frustration.

"You'd better follow your dream, then, if you don't love me enough to come home." Eva was almost in tears, and they were getting close to an argument; she picked up her coat and started to leave.

"Wait a minute, I'll walk you home," he said, disappointed.

They walked back to the farm in silence; after a curt farewell, she went indoors. "You're home early, had a row?" joked Kath. "Oh my goodness, you have, haven't you?" she said, when Eva burst into tears.

"He wants us to move to England and start a new life there," she sobbed.

"Who wouldn't, given half a chance, what's stopping you?"

"Here, this place, the people, Mam and Dad… I can't do it."

"You haven't seen the place yet; give it a try! You can come back if you don't settle," urged Kath, as Tom came downstairs.

"Try what?" he asked, noticing Eva was upset.

"Dai wants them to move to England, and Eva won't go," explained Kath.

"Have you gone quite mad? Have you any idea how many people would like to be in your shoes? If leaving Mam and Dad is the problem, I'll tell you now they'd want you to take this opportunity, I'm certain of it."

"Come on," said Kath, "Let's see what they have to say."

Kath and Eva crossed the yard and went through the little gate that led to Stan's and Nancy's new bungalow.

"Oh dear, what's up? Come in," Stan said, leading them into the lounge where Nancy was listening to the wireless.

"Good heavens, child, whatever's the matter?" she declared when she saw Eva's face.

"Dai wants them to move to Leicestershire after they are married," answered Kath.

"Could do a lot worse," encouraged Stan. "Leicestershire's not so very far away." He understood what was driving Dai; it was a wonder he didn't want to go farther, and emigrate to one of those new countries.

Nancy's feelings were mixed; the last thing she wanted was for Eva to move away, and yet she saw the sense of it, not just for Dai but for Eva too. She could get a very good job there, and before long they should be able to buy a home of their own.

Stan said, "If you want to marry Dai, I think you should go; the worst thing you can do is give him an ultimatum to stay and have him regret it. If you go and can't settle, at least you'll have tried; I'm sure he'd move back if you were unhappy."

Nancy was thinking about the Aarons. "Eva, when your mama and papa sent you to Britain, it was to ensure you had a life. I think you should think of the sacrifice they made, and seize every opportunity that comes your way. I think you should go. You can spend your holidays here in Wales, and we can come and stay with you sometimes."

"If it's our permission or blessing you need, you have it," encouraged Stan.

"Sleep on it," said Kath. "Come on, it's getting late; let's see how it looks in the morning."

Mary could tell by Dai's crestfallen face that things hadn't gone well. "It's not that I don't understand how she's feeling, because I do; but I can't see the life I want for us here," he explained.

"I think you both need more time," she said. "It's all right for you; you've spent time away from here, she hasn't. I think you're being hasty; spend some time back here and get used to civilian life first. If you settle, all well and good; if not, move away, but go steady, you've plenty of time."

Dai knew Mary was making sense; she always did. He saw an option. "I'm going to speak to Mick at the haulier's and ask if he's got a job for me at the yard."

Next morning Dai went to see Mick in his office and asked if he had any vacancies. "I have two, one is driving, the other is maintenance; if I took you on as a mechanic, I'd need you to help with deliveries at busy times as well."

Dai could not believe his luck, and accepted the mechanic's job—all he needed to do now was find somewhere to live. He made his way to the Post Office to see if there were any advertisements on the noticeboard; Gwen Price handed him a post card, "Here's one; Bill and Pauline Davies have a room they want to rent."

"I like the thought of lodging there, it's only a few doors from Mary's. Thank you, Mrs. Price, I'll go and speak to them now."

Pauline Davies opened her front door. "Hello Dai, come in; Mary said you'd returned home."

"I've just accepted a job at the goods depot, and now I'm looking for somewhere to live. Mrs. Price said that you have a room to let."

"Yes, we have; it's the back bedroom. Come and have a look." They went upstairs and she showed him the room. It was identical to Ethel's. "It'll be cosy in the winter, because the immersion heater's in that cupboard."

"I'd like it from today, is that all right?"

"Of course it is; the room's yours if you want it."

He went back to Mary's. "I'm all fixed. I've got a job at the depot, and a room at Mr. and Mrs.Davies's."

"Crikey! Fast worker," laughed Mary. "What are you going to do now?"

"I'm going to take my things to the Davies's, then I'm going to meet Eva when she's finished work. I saw her briefly at the depot when I spoke to Mick; I've told her I've got a job, but she doesn't know I've got digs as well."

"Bring her back here for tea, and you can use the sitting room afterwards; we'll stay out of the way," she offered.

"Thank you, what would I do without you?" He gave her a warm smile, then went upstairs to gather his belongings.

Eva was relieved to see Dai looking happier and less troubled. "How did you get on, did you find somewhere?" she asked.

"I did, at Bill and Pauline Davies's, a few doors from Mary."

"I know them; they have a son who's recently joined the RAF. I suppose they find the house empty without him."

"It's chilly isn't it?" said Dai. "Shall we go back to Mary's? She said we could have the sitting room."

Mary thought it wouldn't be long before they turned up; she switched on the electric fire and took them some tea and biscuits.

"There now, you tuck into these. There's some records in that box if you want to use the radiogram; we'll have tea at about six o'clock, when Mam and Ethel get home from work."

"Are you happy, Dai?" asked Eva. "I mean, are you disappointed to be coming home?"

"How can I be disappointed? I have my family, my friends, a job and a place to live, and, most of all, I have you. Forever, if you'll have me." Taking her into his arms, he said, "I've loved you all my life; all I wanted was the best for us both."

Eva said, "You'll never know how much I've agonised over this. Barbara said I was selfish; she said everyone had always bent over backwards for me. She told me that before I started school, Miss Hughes arranged for Kath and Mabel to support me. Mary made a pinafore dress for me while I was on the boat, did you know that?" Dai shook his head, he had no idea that Mary had been involved, although he wasn't surprised in the slightest.

"Barbara said that the Morgans treated me like a goddess; she said that everything at the farm evolved around me. She reminded me that Kath gave me her bike, and Tom made it like new for me. And now, I have you giving up the life you wanted," she continued, close to tears.

"Come now, don't get upset," said Dai, holding her tighter and kissing her hair. "Everyone knew your circumstances, they just wanted to make things nice for you that's all. Barbara calls a spade a spade; perhaps she just meant to give you a jolt."

"She certainly did that. I've gone over and over what she said, and I don't like myself very much; I think I should do as she suggests, and start giving something back."

"Don't be too hard on yourself. You may not like yourself at the moment, but everyone else does. In fact, I think I'd better put a ring on that finger before someone beats me to it, don't you?" he said taking her left hand and kissing it. "Marry me, Eva, next year, when we've got a bit saved."

"Yes! Yes, I will—let's have an autumn wedding. September next year would be perfect. We could rent a flat to start with, and after a couple of years, if we can afford a mortgage, we could think about buying a home of our own; but we won't buy one until we've looked at houses and jobs in Leicestershire. What do you think?"

"I think you will be a perfect wife and you'll make me very happy."

"Come here," she said, pulling him onto the settee and kissing him passionately; they lay together talking about their wedding and their hopes for the future.

"Shall we go and tell Mary?" whispered Dai.

"Oh, I think we should."

"Hello, you two," said Mary, noticing their flushed, excited faces, she was preparing tea and hadn't expected them to emerge yet.

"We wanted you to be the first to know. We're engaged!" said Dai holding Eva close.

"Congratulations! I can't tell you how pleased I am," Mary was beside herself. "Have you set the date yet? Are you having a long or short engagement? Oh, my goodness! Give me time to make the dresses, won't you?" They all laughed because the usually controlled and clear thinking Mary was all a-fluster. "What about the Morgans? You'll have to ask Stan for her hand, you know."

"She's a grown woman, I don't need to ask for her hand," he laughed.

"Oh yes, you do! You may have been away from the valley, but no one else has, so you'd better get yourself over there."

"Let's go now, before tea," suggested Eva.

"All right, I'll go while I'm feeling brave," said Dai. "Don't forget, there's Glynn and Tom as well as Stan!"

"Go on with you, they'll wonder what took you both so long," laughed Mary. "Why not ask everyone if they'd like to meet at the Collier's tonight for a celebration drink? Mam won't want to go to the pub, but I'm sure she'll babysit if Kath wants to go."

The Morgans were overjoyed, especially when they knew that the couple weren't planning to leave the village for the foreseeable future. Both families met later to celebrate, and were joined by Barbara and her parents; everyone had an opinion about the venue and the honeymoon, and there was laughter when someone pointed out that it seemed to be everyone's wedding except the bride and groom's.

When the evening was over, Dai and Eva said goodnight at the farm gate. "Happy?" he asked.

"You'll never know how happy I am; this has been the best day of my life, and I can't wait to become Mrs. Dai Jenkins."

Chapter Ten
1955

Stan's new copy of The Farmers' Weekly had just been delivered; as the frost was still quite thick on the ground, he decided to have a quick look at it, before going to the village for more supplies.

Nancy came in from tending the geese and chickens with their grandson in tow; she removed his wellingtons and unzipped his siren suit, and she was surprised to see Stan reading his magazine. "Aren't you going to the store?" she asked.

"I was about to go when my magazine arrived, I was having a quick flick through it when this advertisement caught my eye. A sheep farmer from New Zealand is on attachment in the Yorkshire Dales, and he's looking for a few months' work on a Welsh farm. Apparently, he's looking at all aspects of British farming methods and needs some hands-on experience in a challenging climate."

"He'd certainly get it here," laughed Nancy.

"We could do with some help with the lambing; would we be able to put him up, do you think?" he asked.

"Yes, although I think the farmhouse would suit him better if Kath doesn't mind. Eva said she would quite like to move in here until the wedding; if she did, he could have her room. Let's ask the others; if everyone's in agreement, you can reply with an offer for him to come here."

Kath agreed that the visitor could have Eva's room; she hadn't mentioned it to the rest of the family yet, but she was fairly certain that she and Tom were expecting their third child. If they were, the baby would be due at the end of October, and the room would be needed for Paul. Stan replied to the advertisement , and said that he was welcome to stay there, on the understanding that it was until the end of September. Within three weeks, John Flynn was on his way from Yorkshire.

Kath heard the sound of a motorbike coming up the lane; when it arrived in the yard, the rider switched off the engine and stood it on its stand. A large, ruddy-faced man removed his gauntlets, helmet and goggles, and looked toward the back door as she opened it.

Glynn heard the motorbike too, and was crossing the yard to greet him. "John Flynn? I'm Glynn Morgan; my father answered your advert. Come inside and warm yourself."

Kath was standing in the porch waiting to welcome their lodger. "Come in, my name's Kath, give your gear to Glynn and sit by the fire while I make you a drink. We weren't sure what time you'd be arriving. I hope you're hungry; there's shepherd's pie made with our own lamb, and Bramley apple pie for afters. We thought you'd like something Welsh and something English." *He looked so cold, he must have left Yorkshire hours ago,* she thought. "Did you make the journey in one go?" she asked.

"No, I stayed overnight in a bed and breakfast near Stafford; I was late getting there and missed dinner last night, although I did get some breakfast this morning."

Kath gave John a mug of tea and some biscuits to keep him going until dinner time. "Glynn's gone to tell his brother Tom you're here; Tom is my husband, their parents live in the bungalow."

When he had finished his snack she took him to his room, "I hope you don't mind flowered curtains and wallpaper; this was my sister-in-law's room. She's moved into the bungalow until she gets married in September. The bathroom is just across the landing; make yourself comfortable and join us when you're ready."

By the time John had washed and rested on the bed for a few minutes, everyone was gathered in the kitchen. Kath's shepherd's pie was cooking in her new electric oven, and the apple pies were in the range, because Nancy insisted that no electric oven could cook pastry to that standard.

"My, something smells good," said John as he entered the kitchen. Stan stepped forward and introduced himself and Nancy. While they waited for Eva and Dai to arrive, John noted who was who. Glynn, the eldest son, who lives in the bothy and is interested in rugby, the choir, and the farm. Tom, the youngest son, who is married to Kath and is father to Paul and Sally. Stan was born in this house, and brought Nancy to live here after their wedding in 1922. Finally, Eva and her fiancé Dai who are getting married in September.

"They won't be long; Eva's getting ready, and Dai will be on his way," said Nancy, looking through the kitchen window. "In fact, I see them coming now."

"How long do you intend to stay over here?" Tom asked John.

"About ten months, if I've covered everything; I've been working on a farm in the Dales since early January. If I need longer I'll go to Devon—if not, I'll go home. After I graduated from college, I spent three months on a station in Australia and came to England in the new year."

"You've come at a good time; lambing is a few days later this year. It was a slow start, but it'll be all hell let loose within a fortnight," said Glynn.

"I need to be in the thick of it because I want to see the traditional ways of doing things, especially when it goes wrong. I have the theory, all I need now is some British experience; Welsh in particular, because Welsh lamb is among the finest in the world. My father asked me to look at different breeds while I'm here, because our terrain varies; getting good stock for the lowland is no problem, but we own quite a lot of high ground too, so I'm keen to see which breeds graze best on yours."

"I think you'll enjoy being here, John, although no doubt you'll find the weather challenging compared to what you're used to; it can make life very difficult, especially during the lambing season, but we farmers pull together when we can," said Stan.

John told them about his father's ranch in New Zealand and its two thousand acres of excellent grazing pasture, forest and scrubby highland. The fact that the nearest town was a few miles away meant that they tried to make the ranch as self-sufficient as possible; he told Nancy that they didn't have goats on their farm, and that he'd be interested in hers, and the produce she made.

Glynn finished his apple pie and made a move. "If you'll excuse me, I'm going to get back to the ewes; I think there'll be about six births tonight."

"Shall I come with you?" offered John.

"No, thanks, I'm not expecting any problems. Get a good night's rest; there'll be plenty of other nights when you'll be needed."

Stan had to be up early to relieve Glynn in the lambing shed. Tom had winter-damaged walling to repair on high ground, before the sheep could be taken up there for the summer months. Kath had to take Paul to school, look after Sally and provide everyone with meals. In addition to her usual tasks, Nancy was on standby to take care of any sickly lambs; she suggested that they call it a day and have an early night.

As was usual, at this time of year, the entire focus on the farm was in the lambing shed; Nancy made a night shift rota for the men, to ensure that someone was always in attendance. This season had been quite mild; there was the usual wind and rain, but no sleet or snow, which was a bonus, because it meant that the ewes and their lambs could be put out to pasture.

After a few weeks, John gained good insight into rearing sheep the Welsh way. Some of the methods were archaic, and would be invaluable if modern methods or machinery failed. He learned a great deal from Stan; he went to the livestock markets with him when he sold his older ewes and wethers, and joined in the debates over which rams to buy or sell. He saw different breeds, some better suited to certain terrain than others, and learned how the British Government and farmers dealt with anthrax, foot and mouth, and other much feared diseases.

One Saturday morning in May, he saw Barbara arrive at the bungalow; he quickly strode across the yard to a place where she could see him. "Hello there!" he hailed.

"Hello, John," she replied and went over to speak to him. "I've come to be measured; I'm going to be Eva's chief bridesmaid. Dai's sister is making the dresses and she's coming this morning with some material and patterns."

"I'd better let you get on with it, then; how long do you think you'll be?"

"A couple of hours at least, I should think. Why?"

"I wondered if you'd like to go for a spin on the bike this afternoon; I thought we could head down to the coast and you could show me the Gower Peninsular. I understand it's very beautiful."

"I'd like that; I'll make some sandwiches and a flask of tea, I should be ready by about one o'clock if that's okay?" John said it was, and that he would call for her then.

Barbara entered the bungalow with her face aglow; she knocked on the lounge door and walked into the room. There were piles of fabric swatches and dress patterns on the carpet; Mary was sitting on the settee with Eva kneeling on the floor by her side, comparing ivory silk with white lace. "Come and look at all this lovely material," Eva said, and then asked, "Why is your face flushed; have you been running?"

Barbara laughed. "No; I have a date with the man of my dreams."

"Who's that, then?" asked Mary.

"It'll be John Flynn; it is, isn't it?" said Eva, addressing Barbara.

"It is, we're going to the Gower on his motorbike this afternoon."

Nancy said, "He's quite a catch, but don't forget he's leaving in September, and he'll be back in New Zealand before Christmas."

Mary spread the dress patterns over the floor and said, "Let's choose the bridal gown first, then the bridesmaids' dresses and the fabric. Eva, would you like a traditional or modern style?"

Eva looked at the patterns, and was thoroughly confused; she found it hard to choose between the different styles of ballerina, traditional long length, full skirted, and slimline.

"May I make a suggestion?" said Nancy. "If you like them all, consider the season and the venue."

"I agree," said Mary. "It could be windy and likely to feel chilly; if you have a traditional dress, you'll need a long veil and a large bouquet to go with it, not ideal on a blustery day. Also, you'll need higher heeled shoes which will make you taller than Dai, and walking on the chapel's cobbled path could be tricky." She waited a moment while they considered. "On the other hand, if you wore a ballerina-style dress, you could wear shoes with just a tiny heel."

Barbara added, "What about a small veiled hat and a short jacket, or bolero? A posy of roses, or a small white Bible with flowers on the front would complete the look perfectly." Eva imagined herself, and liked what she saw in her mind.

Barbara was for the modern look; she was slightly taller than Eva, and very slim; that style would suit her too. The other bridesmaid was Jenny, Dai's five year old niece. They all agreed that a shorter length dress would be better for her too. The decision was made; the dresses were to be ballerina-style, with a bolero.

"Let's choose the fabric," Mary said, putting the chosen pattern to one side. She was going to use the same pattern for all the dresses and boleros, with more detail on Eva's.

"What colour would you like for your dress, Eva?"

"White, I think; I hadn't considered anything else."

"You could have pale pink, pale blue, ivory, or creamy lemon," Mary suggested. Eva was doubtful, so she continued. "How about white, with pale ivory underskirts and an ivory lace bolero?"

"I like this," said Eva, holding a sample of very light pearl satin. "If I chose this one, and had white net underskirts, would you be able to make a white satin bolero with pearl lace over the satin?"

"I could, but what about this?" Mary passed Eva a piece of beautiful pearl brocade. "Just imagine a bolero made of this with pearls stitched on."

Nancy said, "This is lovely, so luxurious, and perfect for an autumn wedding. I would have the petticoats in pearl net; I think this is much prettier than white."

"It would make a beautiful bridal outfit," said Mary. "But bear in mind, if we have the bridesmaids' dresses and the page-boy outfit in this material, it's going to be very expensive."

"That's all right; Stan's paying, he said she's to have whatever she likes," said Nancy. "What do you think, Eva?"

"I love the satin and brocade."

"I've just had a thought," said Nancy. "My wedding dress was off-white satin, 1920s style. If you like the thought of wearing an heirloom, I'd love you to have it; there's plenty of material in the skirt, and I'm sure Mary would be able to alter it."

"What a lovely thought; is it in the loft?"

"Yes, it's in one of the trunks. I know exactly where it is, if you want to fetch it."

Eva got the step-ladders and climbed into the loft; she found the dress and passed it down to Nancy. When they returned to the lounge, they removed the protective packaging, and a whiff of camphor wafted in the air.

"Moth balls!" exclaimed Barbara, amused.

"Oh dear, it's been in the same trunk as my old fur muff; I didn't want the moths to get at it."

"Not to worry, I've dealt with worse smells than this; I'll put it in a bag with some baking soda and hang it in the fresh air, that should see to it," said Mary, admiring the dress. "Isn't it beautiful? It seems such a pity to alter it. You know this shade of white is almost the same as that pearl satin, isn't it?"

"Shall I slip it on?" asked Eva.

"Yes, let me help you," Nancy started to undo the buttons on the dress, while Eva pulled off her skirt and jumper. When all the fastenings were undone, Nancy and Mary gently lifted it over her head and adjusted it into place.

Nancy fastened the dress, while Mary took her tape measure and pins from her sewing box; she looked at the picture on the chosen pattern and pinned up the skirt to the correct length. She held out the front and one side of the skirt, and asked Barbara to do the same with the other side and the back.

"I'm doing this to give me an idea of how many layers of net will be needed to hold the skirt out."

Having decided how much net she required, Mary cast a critical eye over the bodice. "It's too baggy; it needs four short darts adding at the front, and two long ones at the back."

Eva was delighted. "Shall we have a look at the brocade swatch next to the dress? It'll give us an idea of what the bolero will look like." When Mary held the swatch against the dress, Eva said, "It's perfect; the shading in the brocade matches the dress perfectly. I love it, but are you sure, Mam?"

"Definitely! It would give me such a lot of pleasure to see you wear it on your wedding day."

Choosing the fabric for the bridesmaids' dresses was easy; they chose satin, and the same brocade as the bride's bolero. Eva said, "I like deep dusky rose; I think it would suit both Barbara and Jenny, with their dark hair."

"I think so too; it's a nice end of summer, early autumn colour. What about these?" Mary asked, handing the rose brocade and satin swatches to Eva.

"Perfect; what do you think, Barbara?"

"I love it. What about the page's outfit? We can't dress Paul in this, can we?" laughed Barbara.

"That's no problem," said Nancy. "His trousers can be made of pearl satin, his waistcoat of pearl brocade, perhaps with a rose cummerbund?"

"I think I'll make a pearl cummerbund as well, just in case." Mary thought a rose one would complement the bridesmaids' dresses beautifully, but she was doubtful whether Paul would wear it; she had made a lot of page-boy outfits in her time, and it often became problematic when it got down to choosing the colour.

"Is that it, have we done? Are you happy with your choice, Eva?" asked Nancy.

She said she was delighted with everything. "Sam will be arriving soon with Jenny; shall I make a pot of tea before we take the measurements?"

While Eva made the tea, Nancy and Mary went to the farmhouse to find Kath. She took them, armed with a tape measure and note pad, to where Paul was playing with his fort and soldiers.

"Paul, stand up a minute, while Miss Jenkins measures you for your outfit," said his mother. The measuring was swift, and he was soon on the floor again, with his soldiers.

"There's no point taking exact measurements at the moment, because he'll grow between now and September; but it'll give me an idea of how much fabric to order," said Mary.

She returned to the bungalow with Nancy, and measured Eva and Barbara; when Jenny arrived, she took an approximate measurement of her, too.

"That's it, we're done for now," she said, packing her things away.

"I'll take you home, if you like," offered Sam. "Would you like a lift up the lane, Barbara?"

Barbara changed into slacks, a warm sweater and a pair of flat shoes; she had no idea what time they would get back, so she took a jacket as well. She was ready when John arrived; she gave him the sandwiches and flask, and he put them into the bike's storage compartment. She climbed on to the pillion, he mounted the bike, and they were off.

Down green lanes they sped to the main road, through Neath and Swansea, and along the seafront to The Mumbles. John parked his bike near the pier, and they drank their tea and ate their sandwiches on a nearby bench.

He told her about his life in New Zealand, and his three sisters still living at home. He told her about the hard life his grandparents had experienced in Ireland while trying to eke out a living on a small holding near Killarney, and their move to Christchurch, where they laboured on a sheep farm until they had enough money to buy a small flock of their own.

He explained that demand for fleeces and meat before, and after, the First World War had meant that the farm prospered; by 1945, his father's brothers wanted their own farms, so he bought their shares and they moved away.

He said that, by Christmas, his travels would be over, and he would be back home working alongside his father and building his own house on the homestead.

Barbara told him she had been working in the village woollen mill since she left school. She had started in the carding room, and it had been a filthy, greasy job. Then she had moved on to the spinning and dying area, and now she was a weaver, operating the looms. However, she now wanted to work in the stockroom, where the cloth was stored before being dispatched.

"The stockroom sounds like heavy work to me," said John.

"It is, but I think it'll be better than weaving; the machines are very noisy, and I get the fibres all over me."

"We have a lot in common, don't we?" John said. "I produce wool, and you process it."

"Yes, we do, although I couldn't do what you do; it breaks my heart when the Morgans take the lambs away from their mothers, ready for the market next day. They bleat for hours on end; it's horrible."

"I used to get upset when I was a nipper, but you get used to it, especially if it's your living."

"Eva said the same; it used to upset her, but I don't think she notices any more."

Changing the subject, she asked if he would like to move on and see more of the Gower; he said he would. He helped her on to the pillion and they sped off into the lanes. They stopped and admired the pretty coves, magnificent beaches along the coast, and the interesting strata in the cliffs. John observed the rock face, fascinated by the rise and fall of the different coloured layers in the stack. "I would quite like to be a geologist."

"I think the National Coal Board employ geologists," she offered.

"Not quite what I had in mind," he replied good-naturedly.

On the way back they called for a drink. "I've had a lovely time, thank you," said Barbara, sorry the day was coming to an end.

"I've enjoyed it too; will you come out with me again?"

"Yes, I would like that."

"Are you free tomorrow evening?" She said she was, and they made arrangements to meet after work. After that day, they saw each other every evening and Sunday, and it was clear to everyone that John's return home to New Zealand was going to break their hearts.

During August, John asked Barbara to marry him and move to New Zealand; she said yes straight away. They decided to marry in Wales, in the Bethesda Chapel, three weeks after Dai and Eva; it was to be a simple affair, with Barbara's close family and a few friends present.

"I can't wait, John, it's going to be such an adventure. Mam and Dad have been marvellous about it; I know they're going to miss me, but they see the opportunities and want the best for me. I saw my old head mistress the other day, she was so pleased she hardly knew what to say; she always encouraged her pupils to spread their wings and move to pastures new. I'll bet she didn't think I'd be one of them!"

Chapter Eleven

Dai and Eva's wedding day dawned with a September mist hovering low in the cwm; the sun was just beginning to peek over the eastern hills. *It's going to be a glorious day,* thought Stan as he strode across the yard; he was going to get dressed for the wedding in the farmhouse, along with his sons and John Flynn.

When he was ready, he returned to the bungalow, and was overwhelmed at the sight of Eva; she looked wonderful in Nancy's remodelled dress and the bolero with hand stitched pearls on the rich brocade. She wore a tiny hat with a small veil, her shoes were made of ivory leather with a tiny heel, and she carried a posy of dark pink flowers.

Stan and Eva had a few moments alone together while they waited for the car to return from the chapel. Dai and his best man Sam were already there, chatting with the guests. Nancy, the bridesmaids and page-boy were in the wedding car, and on their way.

"You look wonderful, Eva."

"Dad, I…" She couldn't continue; her voice cracked and her eyes filled with tears.

"I know, sweetheart, and you have been the best daughter we could have had. Mam and I are very proud of you."

"There's things I want to say, but I don't seem able to find the words."

"There's no need, we know. Look, the car's arrived; are you ready?"

She nodded.

"Come on my daughter, let's go."

The wedding car arrived at the chapel, where a gathering of local women were waiting to see the bride. Eva got an applause and a hail of good wishes when she stepped out of the car. After a brief moment in the porch, Stan escorted Eva down the short aisle, followed by Jenny and Paul under the watchful eye of Barbara who was walking behind them.

Reverend Pritchard conducted the service; it was almost sixteen years since he had welcomed Eva to the chapel, and it was he who baptised her shortly after the dreadful news of her parents. Of course, all his weddings were special, but there was something extra special about this one. For a brief moment, he imagined the frightened evacuee looking up at him—now he saw a beautiful confident young woman. He looked at Dai, once a bright little star at school, then the scruffy down-at-heel teenager, who had turned into this smart and handsome man standing next to his bride.

While everyone settled, he lifted his gaze and looked across the congregation: there was Miss Hughes, looking as lovely as ever in a navy suit, pink blouse and matching hat. *Why had she never married? It was beyond him – didn't his wife once say there was someone and she lost him in the First World War?* There was Bob and Madge Lewis watching their daughter take Eva's posy and checking that the two little ones were standing to attention.

On his right were the Morgans; when he had first arrived in Manddiogel, Stan and Nancy had been a young married couple. Now they had two grandchildren and another on the way. Dai's family were on his left; his mother, Emily Jenkins, was in the front row with her daughters, Mary and Ethel. Her son Sam, the best man, was standing next to Dai; Sam's young daughter Jenny was standing in the aisle behind the bride. *How proud Mrs. Jenkins looks, it's such a pity Gil Jenkins didn't live to see today.*

He took the bride and groom through their vows, and the harpist accompanied the congregation when they sang 'Calon Lan' and 'Praise, my Soul, the King of Heaven'. It was a relaxed and happy congregation that emerged into the autumn sunshine.

"Wasn't that a lovely service, Mary?" said Ethel. "I think you made a wonderful job of the outfits; I love the mens' tartan waistcoats."

"Thanks, Ethel. It won't be long before you're making tailored garments too; you're quite capable," replied Mary while watching the photographer. "I think we'd better move over there; it looks as though we're needed for a group photograph."

The reception was held in the village hall; a buffet had been chosen because of the various work demands of the guests, and their need to be able to come and go. Not everyone could have the whole day off, especially not those with farming commitments or shifts at the colliery.

Glynn took Dai and Eva back to the bungalow to get changed into their travelling clothes, and collect their suitcases for the honeymoon. They went back to the reception briefly to see their guests again, before he took them to Bridgend Station.

They chose Tenby for their honeymoon, and stayed in a hotel on the Esplanade with lovely sea views to Caldey Island. The weather was settled, and they spent their time relaxing and exploring the area.

After the honeymoon, they moved into the flat above the recently opened newsagent's shop. Soon afterwards, Dai heard that the colliery was looking for volunteers to support the rescue team in the event of an emergency; although he hated the thought of being in the mine again, he put his name forward. But Eva was concerned. "I understand you wanting to do it, but it's so dangerous; you might be seriously injured."

"Those men are at risk every moment they're down there; they need to know that in an emergency there'll be a quick response. I'd go anyway if I heard the siren, so I may as well put my name on the list."

Barbara and John's wedding day arrived on a pleasant, slightly cooler autumnal day. Mary had made Barbara a suit in pale blue jersey which would come in handy in the future. She borrowed a hat, and carried a small white Bible; she asked Eva to get each guest to sign a page, so she would be able to look at their names in years to come.

Their wedding took place in the Bethesda Chapel and the reception was in the village hall, although they were able to stay with their guests until the end, because they weren't having a honeymoon. Dai and Eva let them have their flat for the weekend while they stayed with Stan and Nancy; afterwards the newly-weds moved into Felin Fach with Barbara's family until it was time to leave for New Zealand.

Madge was up early after a sleepless night on the dreaded day; she had butterflies in her stomach, and her legs felt weak. Until now, she had been strong and supportive of her beloved daughter's decision to move to the other side the world, but today she was in pieces. In an attempt to hide her feelings, she tried to keep busy and cooked a special breakfast for everyone.

This has got to be right, she thought. *Look at my daughter's face, radiant with love for her new husband. What would her life be like here, married to a local lad with few prospects and working in that dusty mill until the babies came along to drag her down? John came from a prosperous and loving family who were looking forward to welcoming her into their home. Barbara has made a wise decision, at least in the material sense.*

The train from Cardiff to Southampton was due to depart during the afternoon; there had been some debate about family and friends going to the station with them, but everyone said they felt more comfortable with the thought of saying their goodbyes in the privacy of Felin Fach.

Throughout the morning, friends and well-wishers came to say farewell. Madge was pleased because the visitors lifted her spirits. The last visitors were Eva and Nancy; they arrived about an hour before Barbara and John were due to leave.

Eva and Barbara went upstairs to Barbara's bedroom for some last moments together. Nancy could see Madge was struggling, and offered to make a pot of tea, tears ran down her face while she watched Nancy fill the kettle. "You know," said Nancy, "you need to be ever so brave; do try to have her last memory of you smiling and waving."

"I will Nancy; I couldn't bear it if I made it difficult for her to go. Will you come back later and spend the afternoon with me?"

"Of course I will."

Upstairs, Eva and Barbara were sitting on her bed, holding each other's hands.

"We've spent some hours in here, haven't we?" said Barbara sadly.

"You're my first and best friend Barbara; I can't tell you how much I'm going to miss you. Do you think we'll ever see each other again?"

"Oh yes; John says we'll come back for visits. We should write to each other at least once a month; shall we promise to?"

"I promise," said Eva. "I think we ought to go downstairs now; it's almost time for you to go."

"We'll leave you now; the taxi will be here soon," said Nancy, gathering her coat and bag. "Are you ready, Eva?"

"No," she said tearfully. "All the very best of luck, Barbara; be happy, and don't forget us." She gave her best friend a long hug, and reluctantly let her go; then she kissed John on the cheek, and said, "Take good care of her, John."

He nodded. He loved his new wife so much and it hurt to see all this sadness; but his own family and a new life was waiting for them in New Zealand.

Eva and Nancy left Felin Fach; by the time they had crossed the leat, they were both in tears. "Do you need to get back to work?" asked Nancy.

"No, I took the whole day off; I'm working on Saturday instead."

"Do you want to come home with me until I go back to Madge's? I said I'd spend the afternoon with her." Eva went back to the farm and spent the rest of the morning there; after a light lunch she walked up the lane with Nancy, then slowly made her way back to the flat.

Barbara cried most of the way to Cardiff Station. John held her hand, while the taxi driver talked to them, and listened to their plans. On arrival at the station, she washed her face and rallied slightly; by the time the train had crossed the border into England she was getting into the spirit of the adventure.

From Southampton station, a taxi took them to a small hotel near the docks just in time for a late dinner. The following morning, they checked out of the hotel and made their way to the quay. Barbara was in awe of the enormous ship bound for Christchurch; she hadn't realised it was going to be so big. When the embarkation procedure was dealt with, she climbed the gang plank quickly, eager to get to their cabin and start exploring.

Hundreds of people were standing on the quay waving to the passengers on board; the ship sounded its horn and slowly edged away from its dock. The tugs escorted it into the Channel and they were on their way.

Chapter Twelve
1960

Dai was servicing an engine in the workshop on a bleak January day; there was some shelter from the force-seven blowing in from the Atlantic, but it was uncomfortably cold.

Suddenly, pulsing in the wind was the sound every mortal in the valley dreads—the Colliery Siren: its desperate wail, soul like, pleading from the depths of hell.

Eva heard it in her office and instinctively ran to the window; she saw Dai run across the yard and out of the gate. She grabbed her coat, and ran down the footpath towards the colliery. When she arrived, people from the cottages were already there; those from the village with relatives on that shift were arriving.

She looked for Dai, but couldn't see him; he must be in the lift that had just gone down. "What's happened?" she asked the nearest person.

"Don't know, fire-damp probably; someone said there was an explosion. There's flooding down there now; some volunteers have joined the rescue team, and the ambulances are on their way."

The lift came to the surface full of filthy and wet distressed men. The doctor arrived and went down into the mine with two more rescuers; the lift continued bringing men out of the mine until the only ones left down there were the rescuers, the doctor, and those who were trapped.

Malcolm Lloyd had been close to the explosion; his hands and face had been badly burned when the coal dust in the air ignited. The doctor gave him an injection to calm him and some emergency treatment for the burns; he was gently lifted on to a stretcher and sent to the surface.

Jim Faulks and Ben Fry had been trapped in rising water; the explosion had made a sizeable crack in the rock and water had gushed in. One of the props had given way, and some of the rock it was supporting had fallen on to Jim and trapped him. The explosion had damaged the water pumping system, and areas of lighting were out; one of the ventilation pipes was fractured, and there were concerns about the escaping methane.

The rest of those missing were found, or had managed to find their own way to the muster. Dai and other rescuers helped the doctor administer first aid to anyone who needed attention before they were able to go into the lift. When confirmation came from the lamp room that everyone was accounted for, most of the volunteers returned to the surface, leaving the professionals to rescue Jim and Ben.

It was chaos on the surface; ambulances were taking the injured to hospital, officials arrived, and the majority of miners with no injuries were making their way home. Reverend Pritchard was giving reassurance to the distressed; he said prayers for the safe recovery of Jim and Ben, and for Malcolm in the ambulance speeding its way to hospital.

Eva was waiting for Dai to arrive at the surface, she watched the lift come up countless times without him; when he did appear he was wet through, covered in coal dust, and suffering pain in his right arm after having slipped on the wet floor. He was taken to hospital, to be checked for gas inhalation and a broken wrist; he returned with his arm in plaster, and thankfully no other injuries. She helped him bathe and change into clean clothes. "I'm going to the Welfare, to see if there's any news; I won't be long."

"Have something to eat first."

"No, I need to go now, I want to see if they've got Jim and Ben out."

"All right; I'll have something ready for when you get back."

He didn't stay long, because he knew Eva was anxious to have him home. "They think a spark from metal ignited escaping gas, and caused the coal dust in the air to explode. Fortunately, the emergency team had a pump, and were able to get the water out quicker than it came in. They've got Jim and Ben out – Ben's ok, but Jim's critical, because he's crushed. Malc has serious burns on his face, and there's speculation that the flash has blinded him."

Eva was aware of the thousands of miners killed in Welsh coalfields during the last one hundred and fifty years. "Two very serious injuries, then; thank God, no fatalities this time." It had been said, probably by the upper classes, in one of their mansions far away, that the rich coal seams in South Wales were a blessing; they might have been, for those building the Empire. She regarded them as a curse.

A month later, on Saturday afternoon, she decided to reply to Barbara's latest letter, while Dai watched Grandstand on the television.

She settled at the dining table and started to write:

Flat 1,
26, St. John Street,
Manddiogel,
Glamorgan,
Wales.

6th, February 1960

Dear Barbara,

Thank you for your last letter, I'm pleased you enjoyed Christmas; I still find it hard to imagine you eating your Christmas dinner outside. How was little Jonathan? Did he take notice, or is he too young still? We spent a quiet Christmas Eve at the flat, just the two of us, and then we went to the chapel for Midnight Mass.

On Christmas Day we went to the farm really early because we wanted to watch the children open their gifts. Paul didn't want a big present; he asked for some more Meccano, and an Airfix kit for his train set. Sally wanted anything horsey, and Lesley got a tricycle. Can you believe she's four now?

There was a serious incident at the mine last month; some gas escaped and there was an explosion. One miner (Malcolm Lloyd) took the blast right in his face; he's still in hospital, and I think he might be blinded. Water poured in, trapping Jim Faulks and Ben Fry, they got Ben out okay, but Jim was crushed under fallen rock. They did all they could at the hospital to save him, but he died from his injuries; he had three sons. His widow is Ginny Price, who used to work at the bakery before the war.

Dai was in the rescue party; while he was in the mine he slipped and fractured his wrist. This latest accident has worried me, and I've been thinking about our future. He's concerned about his job, because it looks as though the company is going to move everything to Cardiff. If they do, I'll lose my job as well, unless I transfer to Head Office. If this means we have to move down there, we may as well give Leicestershire a try. We've saved enough for a deposit on a house, and with no signs of our having a family, I feel I'd like a change. Mam and Dad have their grandchildren now, so I'd feel a bit better about leaving them.

Which reminds me, I saw your Mam a couple of weeks ago. She told me about the marvellous Christmas present you and John bought them. She said John persuaded them to let him pay for the installation and line rental of a telephone; she felt a bit nervous about having one at first, but when your dad explained she'd be able to speak to you, she agreed and is very pleased she did. Perhaps we'll have a telephone when we buy our new house; we'll be able to book a call and have a quick chat.

Dai's sister Ethel is courting strong with one of the drivers who works with Dai. He's a bit older than her, he puts me in mind of Mr. Dick in the David Copperfield story; he's very wise and doesn't speak much, but there's value in what he does say. Ethel told me he's been teaching her to read and write; when I went round the other day, she was reading a book.

I think that's about it for now. Say hello to John, and give Jonathan a cuddle from me.

Love, Eva. xx

She sealed the letter, and put it in her handbag, ready to post on Monday. When the sports programmes were over, and Dai had checked the pools, she served dinner and brought up the subject of moving. "I've been thinking, we want to buy a house and yet our jobs are insecure; I think this might be a good time to consider Leicestershire, what do you think?"

"I'm all for it; I've been hoping that we'd go one day."

"It's going to take some planning, isn't it?"

"We should go at Easter and have a look. In the mean time, I'll write to some of the engineering companies I've been interested in, and see if they have any vacancies. If not, we'll buy a newspaper and see what other jobs there are in the area."

"Should we keep it under our hats until we've been?" she asked.

"We can try, although I think if we go away at Easter they'll catch on."

"Perhaps not, then; we'll tell everyone we're going to see if we like the area and to get some idea of the house prices."

Killorglin
Hawsker
Christchurch
N.Z.

2nd, March 1960

Dear Eva,
I'm very pleased you've decided to think about making a move from the Valleys, although I wish you would consider moving here. There's an abundance of jobs for people like you and Dai to choose from; this country needs more mechanics and women with secretarial skills and you're just the right age. You'd get travel assistance, a job each, and we could put you up until you found somewhere to live. Please say you'll think about it. I'm sure you'd have a good life here; there's new housing estates being built near the town, and British people are arriving all the time.

I've just found out that there's another baby on the way; it's due in August right in the middle of lambing. John says it'll be so manic here that another delivery won't make much difference; it's all right for him, he's not giving birth! He's thrilled, and determined to see it born, although I think the midwife might have something to say about that. I suppose he's delivered so many lambs, it's only natural he wants to see his own baby arrive.

Do you remember the evening we spent with you both when we were fantasising about our owning a woollen mill?

Well, we're going to do it, or at least have a try; it's me really, I need an interest apart from raising our family.

John's too busy to get involved, he sees it more as a hobby for me, but his father's all for it. He's been asking me about the little mill in Manddiogel; I think he imagined me working in one of those 'Dark Satanic Mills', until I told him it was in South Wales with eight workers, not Northern England with hundreds! He's looking at suitable buildings, and he's already found some secondhand machinery. I think that, after a lifetime of selling sheep and fleeces, he'd quite like to get involved with processing wool on a small scale. I'll keep you posted...

Eva continued to read the rest of the letter. She decided not to mention Barbara's plea for them to move to Christchurch because she knew the idea would appeal to Dai, and because it really would be a step too far for her.

***

During Easter, while Eva and Dai were in Leicester, a conversation between Stan and his granddaughter sparked something which altered the farm decades later. Sally decided she didn't want to go shopping with Kath; she wanted to spend the morning with Granny and Bampy instead. She was drawing ballet dancers and horses at the dining table when Stan went over to see. "That's a good drawing, do you like horses?"

She passed it to him for a better look, "Yes, do you like them, Bampy?"

He nodded, "When I was a boy, your Great Bampy had a horse to pull the cart."

She didn't know that. "It lived here, on the farm?"

"Oh yes, we kept him in the field near the chicken enclosure; when the weather was very bad he used to go in the barn. His stall was where Daddy keeps the axes and scythes."

Her brain was in flight. "Do you think Mummy and Daddy would let me have a pony; we've lots of room for one, haven't we?"

"Do you know how to ride a pony?" asked Stan, trying to slow her down.

"No, but you could teach me, couldn't you?"

"I'm afraid not; I was allowed to sit on him sometimes when he was in harness, but no one ever rode him, he wasn't suitable for riding."

"Oh," she said, disappointed.

***

Apart from the occasional visit to Cardiff, neither Dai or Eva had seen so many shops in one place.

They watched with amazement, the customers in Woolworths, impatiently waiting to pay for their purchases at the counters, seemingly unable to catch the busy assistant's attention.

They looked around the city centre on Saturday, and noted the estate agents. On Easter Sunday, they drove through the surrounding villages. Eva thought the countryside was lovely. "It's quite flat, isn't it? It seems strange not to see mountains and valleys."

"I like it; driving is much more pleasurable. She doesn't struggle like she does at home," he said, referring to their second hand Ford Popular.

After an early start, they returned to Wales late in the afternoon on Bank Holiday Monday. "I'm completely shattered, what a long way!" said Dai flopping into his chair.

"Nice though, wasn't it?" remarked Eva putting the kettle on. "Leicestershire, I mean, not the journey."

"I liked everything about it, especially those houses on the new open plan estates," he replied.

"Oh, I loved the new ones; I can imagine us living in one of those."

"Are we up for it then, shall we do it?"

"I'm game if you are; shall we use our summer holiday and go back in July?" Eva was trying to lay some plans down for what looked like a complicated move. "I wonder if our newsagent can get the Leicester Mercury for us; if he can, we'll be able look at the job vacancies and arrange some interviews before we go."

***

Sally's desire to have a pony didn't go away; Tom was uncertain and asked Stan for his opinion. "I don't see why not. There's shelter, plenty of land, and miles of green lanes and old drovers' routes for her to use. She'll need lessons, though. I know someone whose niece runs a pony trekking business from their farm up near Hirwaun on the Merthyr Road, doing very well by all accounts. She takes groups of school children from as far away as England into the Brecon Beacons on pony trekking holidays. I think she charges about eight shillings for an hour's tuition. She ought to have a few lessons first; if she takes to it, we can see about getting her a small cob from the auction."

Tom thought about it and told Sally she could have some riding lessons; if she was any good, he might consider getting her a pony.

On Saturday mornings Stan and Nancy took her to the stables for her lessons. While she was there, they walked with their dogs in the Brecon Beacons, until it was time to collect her and take her home. "What do you think, Tom, is she to have one?" Stan asked, after her seventh lesson.

"I think so; she talks of nothing else from dawn 'till dusk. She's changed her comic from Bunty to My Pony, and she's asked for riding gear for her birthday; I think she's committed."

Stan was pleased, "I wanted Eva to have a pony, but by the time we knew she was staying in Britain, she was ready to start work."

"Do you think you could get it for her, Dad? I have absolutely no idea when it comes to horses."

"Of course, let me know how much you want to spend; it would be nice if she could go to the auction with me and choose one she likes."

It was the first Wednesday of the summer holidays, and Sally was up before dawn; the previous few days had been spent helping Stan clear out the old stall. He white-washed the inside walls, and she cleaned the floor and put down fresh bedding. He made the adjacent area into a tack room, with a huge perch for the saddle, hooks for bridle and halter, and shelves for the saddle soap, cleaning rags and other paraphernalia. He was up early, too. "You're like a child, Stan," teased Nancy. "You're going to enjoy today, aren't you?"

"I am; this reminds me of the day I took Eva to get her chickens, although I must admit that the thought of buying a pony is a lot more appealing than a flock of Bantams!"

"I'll see you later, have fun!" she said, giving him a quick kiss before he left.

He walked across the yard to collect Sally; Tom had already hitched the livestock trailer on to the truck, and, within moments, they were clattering down the lane.

They arrived early at the market; livestock was being herded into pens, feed was being stacked, and men were shouting above the noise, as the place came to life. Sally waited patiently, while Stan gossiped with other farmers until it was time to look at the ponies.

He noticed a bay gelding standing quietly next to a smartly dressed man; he went over and asked,

"Is this your cob?"

"He's my daughter's; she's fourteen and needs a larger one with more go. He's twelve hands and ideal for a kiddie, completely bomb-proof."

"How old is he?" asked Stan, looking at its teeth.

"He's eight; we've had him four years. Lovely temperament, never been known to kick or bite."

Stan looked into its eyes and saw a calmness there, it appeared totally unconcerned about the considerable noise and commotion going on. Sally was falling in love, she was talking to the pony and stroking his muzzle.

"Would the little girl like to sit on him?" asked its owner. Sally nodded and Stan lifted her on to its back, she patted its shoulder and said, "I love him, Bampy."

Stan liked the pony too, and asked, "What's your starting price?"

The owner told him, and said that if they could do a deal, he'd withdraw it from the auction, "There's a reason; my daughter is very upset to be parting with him. She had to make a choice because she's outgrown him; she must either get one more suitable for what she wants to do, or keep this one and not enter any more competitions. She's made her choice, but was in tears when I left this morning."

Stan said, "I'll give you ten pounds over your starting price."

"Make it fifteen, and I'll include the saddle and bridle."

"It's a deal."

"Thank you. We didn't want him to go to a dealer; she'll be very pleased to know he's gone to a novice."

Feeling pleased with his deal, Stan and took the saddle and bridle to the truck and went back for the pony; he could see its previous owner was upset. "You and your daughter are welcome to see him anytime, we're at Gorse Wen Farm just outside Manddiogel."

"Thank you, Mr. Morgan, that's most kind, I'm sure my daughter will want to," he replied, as he passed the certificate and receipt to Stan.

When the pony was safely installed in the trailer, they started their short journey home. "Shall we sing our song, Bampy?"

"Go on then; I'll start, shall I?" replied Stan. "Ten Green Bottles hanging on a wall…"

"Auntie Eva used to say 'vall', didn't she?"

"She did—she was always getting her Vs and Ws muddled."

They arrived home, and everyone gathered in the yard to watch the pony being taken from the trailer to his stall. Tom said, "We'll keep him here for tonight; in the morning he can go into the paddock."

"Has he got a name?" asked Kath.

"Nugget," Sally answered.

"Nugget! That's a funny name; I suppose you could change it."

"No, I like Nugget; he's like a precious nugget of gold."

***

Dai and Eva went back to Leicester. Each had two interviews, one of Dai's with a large engineering company in the city, the other in Loughborough eleven miles north. Both offered him a job at the end of the interview; he chose the company in Leicester which made industrial knitting machines, because getting to work would be easier from wherever they chose to live.

Eva accepted the position as private secretary to a junior partner in a firm of solicitors. She preferred the solicitor's office because she thought a busy office in a large factory might be too daunting.

With just two days left, they explored the villages, getting a feel for the areas they liked best; in the countryside, east of Leicester, they came upon a village named Thornby. They noticed a quiet lane off the village centre; wild flowers were growing in the verges and the summer sunshine illuminated the branches and leaves of the ash trees.

"Let's go down here," said Dai, turning the Ford into the lane. After a couple of hundred yards, Eva noticed a bungalow set back from the road with a 'For Sale' board attached to the gate post. "Look, there's a bungalow for sale; go back." Dai reversed the car, and stopped at the gate.

The garden was at least half an acre, and completely overgrown; the back garden looked as though it was about three times the length of the front. Green paint was peeling off the window frames and the front door, the windows were filthy, and the whole ensemble was a complete and utter mess.

"I love it Dai, it looks so sad and neglected sitting among all those weeds."

"It's got a lot of potential, let's take a closer look." He opened the gate, taking care it didn't fall off its hinges.

They walked carefully along the uneven path to the front door; there were two bedrooms with bay windows on either side of the porch; the kitchen and lounge were at the rear and overlooked the back garden. All the rooms were empty, except the kitchen, which had a few derelict cupboards at least thirty years out of date; the lounge had an old tiled fireplace with an open grate, wallpaper was peeling off the walls, and the woodwork was a miserable shade of mushroom.

"What a dump! I do like it though, don't you?" said Eva.

"Yes, I do, I wonder how much they want for it." They found the estate agent in the city and asked for the details, they booked a viewing at ten o'clock the following morning.

The agent showed them around the property; there were no special features, and all the fittings needed to be replaced because they were either outdated or broken, "It requires complete rewiring, and, as you see, it needs a new kitchen and bathroom. However, there is no damp in the property, and the roof is sound. It's a just short walk to the village, with all its amenities, and there's a bus every half an hour to Leicester."

Dai told him they were due return to Wales and would let him know their decision shortly.

Chapter Thirteen
1964

Dai and Eva bought the bungalow in Thornby; their hard work and patience over the previous four years had turned it into a smart and comfortable home. The front garden now had a lawn, surrounded by countless rose bushes, and trees were planted along the boundary, which, in time, would seclude the property from the lane. The much larger garden at the rear backed on to fields, most of it was lawned, with three herbaceous flower beds and a pond. It was a wonderful, homely place. Nevertheless, summer holidays were always spent with the family in Wales; it was that time now, and they were preparing their annual visit.

***

Nancy woke when daylight started to seep through the bedroom curtains; it was one of those mornings that begin with an early dawn chorus, promising a wonderful day. She slipped out of bed carefully, not wanting to disturb Stan; she pulled the covers back into place and glanced across at him. He didn't seem to be asleep, but neither was he awake. He appeared semi-conscious; something was seriously wrong. She spoke to him and got no response. Nancy ran to the telephone in the hall, rang for an ambulance, and unlocked the front door. She returned; his breathing was irregular and he was becoming distressed. She climbed on to the bed and held him; he calmed a little and looked up at her, a moment later he sighed, and his breathing stopped.

"Has anyone seen Dad yet?" asked Glynn when he returned to the house for his breakfast.

"No, I haven't, I was out early, but I thought I'd have seen him by now," replied Tom.

Kath looked out of the window toward the bungalow, "It looks as though the curtains are still drawn; eat your breakfasts and I'll nip across."

Kath let herself in; it was quiet, apart from the excited scuffling of the dogs in the kitchen. She went to the front bedroom, knocked on the door and opened it. She was taken aback by what she saw; Nancy was lying on the bed sobbing, with her arms around Stan. Nancy looked up and saw the shock on her face, barely audibly she said, "There's an ambulance on its way, but it's too late, he's gone."

Kath rang Tom at the house straight away, when he arrived with Glynn she went back to look after the children. While they waited for the ambulance to arrive, Tom made Nancy a drink and fed the dogs, Glynn decided to ring the doctor. "He's on his way, he said he'll see to everything."

"I'll get dressed," said Nancy, slowly making her way to the bathroom.

The doctor and the ambulance arrived at almost the same time. Doctor Lloyd-Jones took charge of the situation; he spoke to the ambulance men, and they left. He asked Nancy what had happened, and examined the body, "It looks as though he might have suffered a brain haemorrhage; I'm afraid there'll have to be a post mortem."

Nancy went to the farmhouse with her sons as soon as the undertaker left with Stan's body; Kath told them Reverend

Pritchard had been in touch, and he would be coming to see them shortly. In the mean time, Kath telephoned Eva and managed to catch her before she left for work. After she told her the sad news, she handed the telephone to Nancy, and left them to talk awhile.

Eva was devastated, and unable to think; Nancy handed the telephone back to Kath. Eva managed to say, "We'll travel down on Saturday and spend a few days with Mam after the funeral, if you think that would be okay?"

"Yes, I'm sure she'd like that; I'll ring you as soon as we know more." Kath put the receiver back on its cradle, and asked Nancy to stay at the farmhouse. "Come and stay here awhile; let me look after you."

"I think I would like that, just for tonight."

"Of course, you must stay as long as you like." Nancy remained there until Saturday; Kath did some cleaning at the bungalow and got the spare room ready for Dai and Eva.

Nancy felt nervous while she waited for Eva and Dai, and was relieved when they arrived. During the evening, she told them about the past two days. Eva was struggling to take it in and kept shaking her head in disbelief. Nancy asked if she wanted to go with the rest of the family to see Dad at the chapel of rest on Monday.

"Do you mind if I don't?" she replied, knowing she wouldn't cope well. "I'm sure Dai will want to, but I'd rather remember him as he was when I last saw him, smiling and waving as we left after our lovely holiday last year."

"Of course not; you must do as you feel," she said, mindful of Eva's considerable experience when it came to grief.

Stan's funeral day dawned with light rain wafting across the land from the West. His family knew that there was going to be a lot of people attending, so they broke with tradition and chose to hold the service in the chapel rather than at home.

As expected, the chapel was full, friends and farming associates travelled from all over the region and the counties beyond; it was so full that some men had to stand in the porch. This was one of the longest services Reverend Pritchard had ever conducted. Gwen Hughes read from the book of Mathew, and Dai's sister Mary read from John; the hymns 'Blaenwern' ('Love Divine') and 'Cwm Rhondda' ('Guide Me, O Thou Great Redeemer') were sung with the support of the chapel choir, and 'ArHyd Y Nos' ('All Through The Night') was played by the harpist.

After the service, as was the custom, only the men went to the cemetery for the burial; they gathered around the Morgan family plot where Stan's parents and his baby daughter Elizabeth were buried. The Reverend led the prayers, and the coffin was gently lowered into the grave; he said the final prayer of the committal, and the funeral was over. Some drove, but most of the mourners walked through the village and down the lane that led to the farm. Even on a day such as this, the kitchen was a haven and a welcoming place, the only sign that all was not well was the black crepe draped over the back of Stan's comfy leather chair.

The men entered the kitchen and hung their coats on the rack to dry. Kath told them not to worry about the mud on their shoes; the slates on the floor had stood much worse than that. The women had been busy making tea and sandwiches; someone was cutting a cake, and someone else was pouring sherry into glasses.

The sherry went down well, and the mood began to lighten. There was laughter, too, when some of the farmers shared their stories about the goings on at the livestock market and some of the things the animals got up to, especially the time when Charlie Williams's bull had broken loose on its way to the auction ring.

Although it was summer, recent rain had lowered the temperature and dampened everywhere; with that in mind, Tom had made a fire earlier in the front room. The women gravitated to it, and settled in there. The men remained in the kitchen and continued their stories, out of earshot.

Next day, Dai and Eva visited old friends; Nancy thought she would like to go to the cemetery and look at Stan's flowers. She asked Kath if she had time to go with her.

"Yes, I've got time, I'll take you in the car, because it's still damp under foot, and a bit chilly." She quickly cut a large bunch of flowers from the garden, wrapped it in newspaper and put it on the back seat.

Kath parked her Austen on the grass verge, outside the cemetery, they walked down the path to the fresh pile of earth covered with flowers. "Lovely spot, isn't it, just look at that view," said Nancy. "The hours we spent up here, after Elizabeth died…"

The two women looked thoughtfully towards the West; at the land as it sloped gently, hiding most of the village from view. They could just make out the chimneys of Felin Fach, peeking over the ridge. "So many wreaths and arrangements; there's even some from people I don't know," said Nancy, reading each message in turn and noting who wrote it.

"Would you like a little time on your own, while I put these flowers on my family's graves?" Kath asked. Nancy said she would like a few moments, and went to the bench where she used sit with Stan. Her thoughts drifted until they settled at the time when they had first met.

She was twenty, just starting her teaching career in Bridgend when she met Stan; he was twenty-one, and working on his father's farm in the Valleys. They met during the summer when she was staying with a friend whose parents ran a farm near Llantrisant. He had delivered some ewes to the farm in his father's ex WW1 army truck and was having difficulty getting it started. When he finally solved the problem, her friend's mother offered him some dinner before his long drive home; during that meal, they clicked and started seeing each other whenever they could.

In the spring of 1922, they married; Nancy gave up her teaching career, and went to live on Gorse Wen Farm with Stan and his parents. The farmhouse was at least eighty years old, and very uncomfortable. An ancestor, the family thought it was the great-great grandfather, had built the house in around 1830. It was understood that he had been quite senior in the army, and had fought at Waterloo. When he retired from the army, he saved his reward and went into farming; about ten years later he spent the money on building materials and set up his own farm.

Glynn was born in 1923, and was a robust little boy. Elizabeth was born the following year, and, although she had been a healthy baby, she died in her cot one night, for no apparent reason.

Nancy paused her thoughts, and reflected on their baby girl in her tiny coffin, buried beneath those lovely flowers.

She was pleased to see Kath coming back up the path; she was smiling, as usual, and gave a wave as she approached. Kath noticed the tears on Nancy's face, and put her hand on her arm. "He's with his parents and daughter now, albeit too soon."

"Yes, he certainly wouldn't have expected to die at sixty-four; he was always so strong and healthy. You never can tell, can you?"

"No, you can't. I think life, with its twists and turns, is a mystery to us all."

Nancy dabbed her eyes with her handkerchief and said, "When Elizabeth died, I thought my world had come to an end, but gradually I began to function again; I had to, because there was Glynn to take care of, Stan's parents weren't in good health, and their contribution to the farm's workload was diminishing fast. I needed to be a lot stronger than I felt. His parents died within months of each other, which meant he had sole responsibility and could manage the farm in his own way. We had Tom by then; the little boys were so funny, running around all over the place and getting into all kinds of mischief. It was a happy time, and it continued; that's why we were able to offer sanctuary to a refugee. The boys were teenagers at the time and we felt we would cope. Imagine, if you hadn't given Eva your bike, you and Tom might never have married and given us our three beautiful grandchildren."

"I wish Glynn would meet someone; I think he would make a good husband, he's like Dad in many ways isn't he?" said Kath.

"I see a lot of Stan in him, more so than in Tom. Trouble is, he's set in his ways, I can't see him meeting anyone at the rugby or the choir—there's no women there. The rest of his time is spent working. Apart from the livestock market, he doesn't go anywhere; but if he did meet someone, she'd have to be very adaptable."

"Perhaps that's why he's never bothered," replied Kath.

"There was a time, before the war, when he was sweet on Ginny Price; I think he must have been a bit too slow there, because Jim Faulks came on the scene, got her pregnant, and married her."

"I didn't know Glynn used to like Ginny; I worked with her for a while at the bakery. I remember when she and Jim got married. Are you ready to go back now, or would you like to stay a little longer?"

"I'm ready to go; thank you for coming with me."

Chapter Fourteen

The next day, Dai told Nancy that he and Eva were going to visit his family, and asked if she would like to go with them. She said she would; things were getting back to normal on the farm—they had to—but she felt she needed to get away for a few hours.

They called to see Sam first at the smithy; his wife and daughter Jenny were with other women in the village hall, planning Saturday morning's jumble sale. He told them that Jenny was moving up to the grammar school in September.

"Is that the same school Kath and Tom's son Paul will be going to?" asked Eva.

"Yes, that's right," said Sam. "The same one. It was built about three years ago; it has marvellous facilities and buses to transport pupils living more than a mile away."

"Miss Hughes would be in her element, wouldn't she?" remarked Eva.

"I'll say," agreed Dai. "She was a great supporter of further education, before her time, really. Getting a scholarship in our day was one thing, being able to go to the grammar school was quite another."

Sam said, "I think it must be at least five years since she retired; I see her sometimes, she's got a small dog, she often walks past here with it." Eva wondered if they might have time to call round and see her before they returned to Leicester. It would be nice to thank her properly for her part in Dad's funeral; she would speak to Dai about it later.

After visiting Sam, they went to Mary's house. Ethel's fiancé, Peter Harries, was there. "Do you know," Mary told them, "I've never heard Mam laugh so much; he pulls her leg something awful, but she adores him and keeps going back for more."

"Well, she's grist to the mill, see, she's got so many funny ways," said Peter, jokingly defending himself.

"Go on with you. Wait until I'm your mother-in-law; then you'll be knowing about my funny ways," laughed Em.

"Any plans for the wedding yet, Ethel?" asked Eva; the two of them were in the kitchen making tea while Dai got to know Peter better, and Mary chatted with Nancy.

"We're thinking of October, now his old mother's gone; she was a nasty piece of work, and so jealous. You see, Peter's been married before, his wife ran off years ago and took their boy with her. He never saw either of them again; he moved back home when his dad died, and she had him all to herself until I came along. If we'd married while she was alive, there'd be no choice other than to live with her, because she wouldn't have coped on her own. I'm sure she would have made things difficult for us."

They spent the evening together; Nancy remarked how much she enjoyed being in their company. "I've had a lovely time, thank you; I hope the wedding plans go well, Ethel."

"There's not a lot of planning to do because it's going to be at a registry office; we've not booked it yet, but we think it might be in Neath—we're not sure. Anyway, we'll have a modest celebration here afterwards. I'll send you an invitation; I hope you'll be able to come."

On their way back to the farm, Eva mentioned her thoughts to Dai. "Wouldn't it be nice to visit Miss Hughes before we go back to Leicester; do you think we could go tomorrow afternoon?"

"Yes, if you'd like to; give her a ring and ask if she'll be in," he answered.

When they were having an early cup of tea with Nancy, the following morning, they heard a steady clip clop, in the lane. "That's Sally and Nugget coming back. She's always taken him out early, even on school days; they'll go out for a longer ride this evening."

Eva dressed quickly, and joined Sally as she turned Nugget loose in his paddock. "Hi there! Had a good ride?" she asked her niece.

"Yes, thank you. I like to go early, especially in the summer."

"You've had him quite a while now, haven't you?" asked Eva.

"Mum and Dad bought him for my ninth birthday; Bampy took me to the auction and picked him out. That was four years ago last month," she said sadly. "I'm going to miss Bampy; he spent a lot of time with me. If Nugget was muddy after our ride and I had to get to school, he would clean him up for me, and sometimes he helped me muck out and clean his tack."

"I'm going to miss him, too. You know, he and Granny did a wonderful thing for me when I was much younger than you."

"I know you aren't Welsh, and that they gave you a home because you had to leave Germany, but I don't know anything else; will you tell me about it?"

"Yes. Let's sit on those bales over there, and I'll tell you." Eva told Sally all she could remember about her journey to Manddiogel, and how she had met Uncle Dai at school when they were six. She told her about the Bantams, the dogs, Rusty and Meg, and Grace, her little white goat.

"What about your family in Germany, what happened to them?"

"They died during the war. I had a brother; his name was Iwan. He was sixteen when he died. Mama and Papa died the following year." Sally asked more questions; Eva answered as best she could, trying to keep her emotions in check.

"Tell me; where do you ride Nugget?" she asked, feeling ready to change the subject. Sally told her about the bridleways threading through the woods and up to the moors, and the lanes leading to disused clay pits or quarries, which filled naturally with water and became ponds. All were familiar to Eva, especially the ponds; she remembered playing there with Dai and Rusty over twenty years previously.

"We've won some rosettes at the gymkhanas, would you like to see them?"

They returned to the house, and went into Sally's bedroom; Eva went to the window and looked out. She saw Nugget munching grass in his paddock, and the chickens scratching at the earth in their enclosure. Across the other side of the yard was the gate and path leading to Nancy's bungalow. *This used to be Glynn's room*, she recalled. She turned round and saw shelves of trolls with bright hair, a gonk, a Sindy doll, and several soft toys. Pinned to one wall were different coloured rosettes: red ones for first prize, blue for second, yellow for third, green for fourth, and three 'highly commended'. She was impressed. "My goodness, Sally, you have done well, you must be very proud of yourself."

"They're Nugget's really; he's used to competing. The girl who owned him before was always entering competitions with him. She only sold him because he wasn't suitable to move up to the next class with her."

"What will you do with him when you have to move up to a higher class?" asked Eva.

"I'll get a horse, but I won't sell Nugget; I'd never part with him."

"I see—does your dad know about your plans for a horse?"

"Oh no, I haven't told him yet!"

Before they went downstairs, Eva took quick a peek at Paul's room. "This used to be mine," she said, looking at the model cars and strange contraptions on the shelves where her dolls and teddies used to sit. The walls were completely covered with magazine pictures of footballers, rugby players and pop stars; not a square inch of wallpaper was to be seen. Her old desk was still there, an untidy collection of paraphernalia cluttered the top, and temporarily discarded clothes draped from the chair to the floor.

"I think Mum's given up on this one," laughed Sally.

"Never mind; it's still a nice room, for all that."

At two o'clock on Friday afternoon, Gwen Hughes opened her front door, and saw two of her favourite pupils from the past standing there. Eva gave her a bunch of pink and white carnations as they walked into the hallway.

"Oh how lovely, thank you," she said, ushering them into her front room and sniffing the flowers. "Make yourselves comfortable, and then you can tell me all your news. I'll just put these in water; I won't be long." She disappeared for a moment and returned wheeling a tea-trolley loaded with her best china, a pot of tea and a Victoria sponge on a glass cake stand.

"How are you both? I'm so sorry about your father, Eva, it must have been a terrible shock."

"It was, Miss Hughes; we wanted to thank you for your beautiful reading at the funeral."

"Gwen. Please call me Gwen—Miss Hughes sounds so formal, especially now I'm retired."

Eva was looking at an old photograph in a wooden frame on the bureau. Gwen noticed; she picked it up and passed it to her. "This is Freddie, my only love, we planned to marry in 1918 after he qualified, but he was sent to France with a medical team and was killed in Amiens." She sat down and continued. "He was training to be a doctor like his father, but the war dragged on and he joined an army medical corps, I think he escaped being called up in the early stages because of his studies in medicine. But he was young and wanted to fight for his country, so he enlisted and went to France; he hadn't been there long before he was killed near the field hospital where he was working."

They were quiet, at a loss to know what to say. Eva spoke first, "What happened afterwards; what did you do?"

"I was a nurse at the time but after he died, I gave up nursing and became a teacher in Cardiff. My father was a sea captain in what later became known as the Merchant Navy; he travelled all over the world bringing goods back from the Empire. My three sisters and I lived with Mother in a new three-storey Edwardian house, not far from the centre of Cardiff. We didn't see much of Father, but he was loving and caring when he was at home. I was almost sixteen when the war started, and I quickly realised I wanted to be a nurse; I had been well into my training when I met Freddie. Not long after, I was given a post in a hospital caring for badly injured soldiers returning from the battlefields. I thought that's where I'd stay until we married. After the war, I continued nursing until the soldiers either died, were sent back to their families, or went into a home; by that time I was close to a breakdown. That's when Father suggested I choose a more uplifting career. I did, I became a teacher, and when the school in Mandddiogel advertised the position of head mistress, I applied and got the job."

"Oh my, what a lot you've been through; and you never met anyone else?" asked Eva, finding it hard to comprehend why she hadn't married.

"No, I never did. Perhaps if I had remained in Cardiff I might have, in time, who knows? But I have my memories, and this photograph of Freddie, I've always been grateful for that."

Eva nodded with empathy. She looked around the room and noticed that the decor and soft furnishings were modern, but the furniture was heavy and out of date. She could tell it was high quality, and wondered whether some of it might have come from her childhood home in Cardiff. There were interesting objects on the sideboard and windowsills, things she'd never seen anywhere before. Gwen noticed both her and Dai's interest in them, "These were my father's; he brought them back from other countries during his seafaring days. When our parents died, there were many curios to share between us, have a closer look if you wish."

Dai was fascinated by the intricate metal pieces from India, a hand painted china vase from the Orient, and wooden carvings which looked as though they might be African. Gwen explained the origins of each. It was nice to have someone interested in her past; she sensed that people didn't like to ask in case they were seen as prying, or perhaps she gave the impression of being distant.

She wondered about Dai and Eva's lack of children, and thought it a pity that Eva had no blood relative. *Surely there must be someone in Germany, or perhaps Eastern Europe; maybe her ancestors weren't German, she obviously isn't Aryan.* She knew a lot about Dai's family; his ancestors were coal miners decades before she moved to the village, and his siblings and cousins had attended the school while she was head mistress.

After more tea and conversation, it was time to leave Gwen, and return to the farm for their final evening.

On Saturday morning they said their goodbyes. "Better get off now; we'll see you at the wedding in October. We'll give you a ring and let you know when we're home safely." Eva was feeling torn, because a part of her wanted to stay. It was only natural for both of them to feel a fondness for the Valleys, because they had been such happy children there; but she loved their home in Thornby, and was looking forward to going back.

The family waved until they were out of sight. It was always sad when they left, but this time was especially so, because Stan wasn't there. Eva missed his bear-hug, that almost squeezed the breath out of her, and Dai didn't get the handshake from his powerful hand.

"This is going to take some coming to terms with, isn't it, Eva?"

"He's going to be greatly missed by all of us, that's for sure." Their journey home was quiet, both absorbed in their own thoughts of the valley, their families, and their friends.

Chapter Fifteen
1971

Kath put three fresh eggs into a bowl and took them to Nancy's. "Ooo, that's lovely, thank you," said Nancy. "Got time for a cuppa?"

"Yes, I need to talk to you, because I'm worried about something."

"Sit yourself down, and tell me what's bothering you," said Nancy, pulling out a chair for her.

"I'm worried about Lesley; I think she might be ill. I've asked her countless times what the matter is—she just says she is okay and brushes me off."

"What makes you think she's ill?"

"She's very withdrawn, and only speaks when spoken to. She doesn't laugh anymore, and seems to have lost interest in her friends. I'm thinking of going to the school to find out what she's like there."

"Is she eating? She doesn't appear to have lost any weight, does she?" asked Nancy, considering anorexia.

"She's eating normally, although she doesn't want to sit with us at the table; she goes up to her room as soon as she's eaten, saying she's got homework to do."

"Have you spoken to Sally; they're very close aren't they?"

"No, I've not spoken to anyone; I wondered if you would try to find out what's wrong. I know there's something, but for some reason she won't tell me."

"Of course, send her over on some pretext and I'll do my best."

"Thanks, Mam," said Kath, putting her empty cup on the draining board.

Half an hour later, Lesley gave Nancy a cake tin. "Mum's asked me to bring you these flapjacks; she forgot them when she came earlier."

"Thank you, come in. Have you got time to give Granny some company?" she asked, giving her youngest grandchild a hug.

Lesley was pleased to be away from the house, and Mum's questioning, she took the flapjack and glass of orange cordial from Granny and followed her into the lounge. Nancy began with a little small talk; she asked about her friends and how she was getting on at school. Did she intend to stay on longer, as Paul and Sally had?

It was Lesley's reaction to her last question that gave Nancy a clue, because she looked away and stared at the pattern on the carpet.

"Are you being bullied?"

"No Granny, it's not that," she replied, her face reddening and her eyes filling with tears. "I won't be able to stay on at school, I'll have to leave."

Nancy softened her tone as the butterflies welled in her stomach. "Is there any possibility you could be having a baby?"

The dam walls collapsed, and Lesley dissolved into uncontrollable tears. She was pregnant; she thought about four months. "What am I going to do? Mum and Dad will kill me," she sobbed.

"No, they won't; but you're going to tell have to tell them."

"I can't," she wailed, beginning to panic.

"You have to, you've no choice."

"Will you come with me?" she pleaded. Nancy's mind was racing. Tom was at a rugby match with Glynn, and wouldn't be home until much later. Kath, she knew was anxious for news. Sally was busy, and Paul was due to arrive for the weekend at any moment. She picked up the telephone, "Kath, it's me, can you come over?"

Kath ran across the yard, to find Nancy waiting at the back door. "Go into the lounge, Kath, she's in there; I'll stay here."

Nancy sat at her kitchen table and felt quite ill – fifteen years old and pregnant – she couldn't take it in. She thought about her poor daughter-in-law hearing the news at this very moment. *After all the effort she had put into raising her three children: Paul's put his A levels to good use, at university now, studying to be a civil engineer; Sally's finished college and is training to be a riding instructress. Lesley's doing reasonably well and is expected to pass a few CSEs— but what's going to happen to her now? Who was the father, and how old was he?* All these questions were swimming in her head and her heart was pounding.

Kath came to fetch her, "Will you come and join us, Mam? I can't believe this, all the discussions we've had about this kind of thing; I always thought we were close, and yet she couldn't tell me." Kath was more hurt than angry.

"You are close, but she knows your values; telling you this would be nigh on impossible. She's just a child after all," said Nancy.

Lesley was calmer now that Kath knew. "I'm sorry, Mum."

"Who is the father?" Kath asked, dreading the answer.

"He's a boy at school, he's really nice."

"Well, that makes me feel a whole lot better!" she declared sarcastically with her anger rising. "And how old is this really nice boy who's got you into trouble?"

"He's fifteen, he's in my form."

"And are *you* going to tell your dad, or have I got to do it?" she snapped. She walked out of the room, and went into the kitchen where she wept tears of anger and disappointment. Nancy went to her and put her arm around her shoulders, "I know there's nothing I can say of any comfort, Kath, but I will say this: two hours ago you were worried because you thought she was ill. She's not ill, she's pregnant with your first grandchild and what's done is done." *A grandchild*. Nancy's stern words struck home. Kath rallied and went back to her daughter. "Let's tidy ourselves and go home; your dad will be back quite late tonight. I'll tell him when you've gone to bed."

While Lesley washed her face, Kath asked Nancy if she could spend the rest of the day with them. She needed her. "Paul will be arriving from his university soon; no doubt he'll have a lot to tell us."

Paul's grey Mini swept into the yard. He stopped the car, grabbed one of the bags off the back seat, and went into the kitchen. Delicious cooking smells wafted. "I'm starving; I haven't had a decent meal since last time. Hello, Granny." Paul gave Nancy a quick peck on the cheek, and handed the bag to his mum. She pushed his laundry into the Keymatic. "Any more?"

"There's another bag, hang on," he said, and went back to his car.

Nancy watched Kath launder her son's household linen and clothes, listen to Sally's nonsensical girl-talk, keep a watchful eye on Lesley, and cook a meal for five people; she did all that as though nothing had happened.

She doesn't deserve this, Nancy thought; her heart went out to her daughter-in-law. *She has a gift for mothering; no matter what's thrown at her, she always copes; her children adore her, and now there's a grandchild on its way.*

Oh my goodness, I'm going to be a great-granny!

Later, after the rugby match and plenty of heated debates about the game, Glynn and Tom arrived home. Glynn called in quickly to see Paul before going next door to his bothy, Nancy went home, and the family spent a couple of hours together, until Kath encouraged the young people to go to bed. "I think I'll turn in too; are you coming?" asked Tom.

"No, don't go yet, there's something I have to tell you." She told him about the baby, and watched his mood change from disbelief, to despair, and to anger. He actually broke down in tears at one point; he simply could not believe it. His little girl was pregnant; how could she be?

On Monday morning, all hell broke loose; the head master was informed and he told the boy's parents. The father rang Tom and went ballistic, saying his son's life was in ruins, and it was all Lesley's fault. Tom was so angry he slammed the phone down and demanded to know where the boy lived. Lesley told him, and he went to get his car keys. Kath stopped him, and said softly, "Leave it, Tom, there's no point going round there."

"No point? There's every point! I've got a fifteen-year-old daughter expecting a baby! Where's this lad going to be in ten years' time, eh? He'll be married to someone else and starting a family, that's where, and *she'll* be stuck on her own with his kid. I want that supercilious bastard to know just what his son has done to my girl— speaking about her as though she's a back street trollop! I'm not having it!" Tom was enraged; he grabbed his car keys, threw the back door open and stormed into the yard.

Kath snatched the dog's lead off its peg and threw it at him, "Don't you dare get in that car! Take the dog out and calm yourself." Neither had ever seen the other so angry. Tom kicked the lead out of the way and strode across the yard.

Nancy heard the commotion and went outside, she hailed him from her gate, "What's going on? I've never heard such a commotion." Tom was so angry he could barely speak.

"Come inside, and calm down," she demanded. "Now you sit there and listen to me. What's happened is a serious thing, and I can understand how you must be feeling, but it's not a tragedy, and it's not the end of the world. Two very young people have been experimenting, and they've been caught out. She's not an unfortunate Irish girl from years ago who'll have her baby taken away and then be handed over to the nuns. And neither is she one whose father is going to throw her on to the streets to fend for herself. Now, I suggest you pull yourself together and look at the facts. You have a large house with plenty of room, and a loving wife who will support both mother and child. If you calm down and think about it, you'll see that Kath will enjoy looking after the baby while Lesley's at school. I agree, she might be a bit limited in finding someone prepared to marry her with someone else's baby, but that doesn't mean she won't, does it?"

Tom calmed down as she spoke. "I'm trying to imagine how Dad would have reacted in my shoes."

"Oh, I think we both know the answer to that one. He'd accept the fact, and be looking forward to the arrival of his first great-grandchild." She smiled to herself, musing what it would be like if Stan was there with them today—he would wear a serious expression on his face which was supposed to mask his joy at the thought of their first great-grandchild.

The final weeks of Lesley's pregnancy coincided with the annual holidays, and her confinement would be right at the beginning of the school year; the head master said that she need not miss much, because relevant information could be collected from the school.

The boy's parents remained hostile, and were only concerned about the impact on their son. They had ambitions for him which didn't include supporting a child, financially or otherwise; they had no interest in the baby whatsoever, therefore both sets of parents agreed on no financial support and no contact.

"I feel a bit better now all that's sorted out," Kath told Nancy. "Perhaps, when he's older, the boy might want to see his child; we wouldn't want to deprive the baby of its father, but we hope he stays away."

Spring turned into summer, and Lesley finished the school year in a maternity dress. The baby's father moved to another school, and, as agreed, there was no further contact.

Nancy was entering the library when she saw Gwen Hughes leaving with some books, Gwen smiled at her and said, "Hello Nancy, how lovely to see you, how are you?"

"Hello Gwen, I'm fine thank you. I suppose you've heard that my granddaughter is expecting a baby in September?"

"Yes, I did hear; I have no doubt Kathleen will be a very loving and supportive grandmother. She always had a strong maternal streak in her, even as a child."

"She's actually looking forward to it; we all are. It doesn't take away our concerns over Lesley's future, but the baby is going to be very welcome."

Chapter Sixteen

"Will you put this up for me, please?" Dai scrutinised the blue and cream plastic container that Eva was holding.

"What on earth is that?" he asked.

"A tea dispenser!"

"A what?"

"A tea dispenser; it goes on the wall. You put the teapot underneath, press the button, and the correct amount of tea goes into the pot."

"Shall I put it next to the tin opener and all the other gadgets?" *She's got drawers full of cutters, peelers, knives, and things I can't fathom, and yet I've never seen her use anything other than the old knife she's used since we got married.*

The telephone was ringing. Eva answered it and Kath's excited voice came down the line. "It's a girl, Lesley's had a daughter! She's early, but at six pounds and one ounce there's no concerns. She did go into the Cottage Hospital in the end; they thought it best, with her being so young. She's named her Beth, after Tom's sister Elizabeth."

"Lovely news, congratulations! Let us know when they're at home and settled, and we'll come over for a long weekend."

"Will do; look forward to seeing you soon."

Dai was looking sceptically at the tea dispenser when Eva returned to the kitchen, "Lesley's had a daughter; she's named her Beth, after Mam and Dad's Elizabeth. Wasn't that thoughtful? I'll reply to Barbara's letter this afternoon, and tell her the good news."

Amroth,
Shady Lane,
Thornby,
Leicester,
LE7 5HY.

16th, September 1971

Dear Barbara,

Thank you for your letter. It arrived yesterday, and I'm very pleased to hear of Patrick's safe arrival. I love your choice of name – Patrick Flynn – what a fantastic Irish name! Was he named after one of John's ancestors? I think of you often, and imagine you having lots of fun on the farm with your children in that lovely climate, you lucky thing!

Dai and I have been thinking about having a holiday over there, and paying you a visit sometime. It seems ages since you were here last—it was before Rachael was born wasn't it? So it must be at least five years. I imagine it'll be quite a while before you can come again; you can't expect John's mam to look after four, can you?

I have good news, too; Lesley's baby was born yesterday in the Cottage Hospital. She had a girl and she's named her Beth, I think they'll be home soon because she was six pounds and one ounce at birth, and she's doing well. Lesley will be back at school before long, and Kath is looking forward to looking after her new granddaughter. A lot of people have knitted or crocheted baby clothes, and Mary has made lovely sets for the pram and cot. Kath asked her if she would make a christening gown out of her wedding dress; of course, she said yes. Now she knows the baby's name, she's going embroider a fancy B. M. on the bodice. Kath wanted a family heirloom to pass on; apparently it's exquisite.

I've got one more piece of news from the home front: Glynn and Ginny (Price) have been spending a lot of time together. He used to see her at some sort of youth club at the Welfare thirty years ago, just as friends, but she married Jim Faulks and that was that. He wanted to renew their friendship after Jim died in the mining accident, but she was cautious (I think Jim used to knock her about a bit), and with having the three boys to consider, she thought she was better off on her own; but they've all left home now, so she's free to do as she pleases. Mam's a bit concerned; she thinks he's too set in his ways, what with the rugby and the choir, but Kath thinks it'll do him good, so we'll see.

I think that's about all for now. Dai sends his love.

Until next time, Eva xx

"Oh, you've fixed the dispenser, thank you," said Eva, fetching a packet of tea from the pantry. "I'll fill it up and test it." She switched on the kettle, and got the cups and saucers ready; when the water boiled, she warmed the teapot, and placed it on the worktop underneath the dispenser. She pushed the button, and the measured amount of tea came out of the spout and into the teapot.

"What happens if it's too weak—do you press it again and end up with tea that's too strong?" Dai grumbled. "I don't know what's wrong with our old caddy. You can keep a spoon in it; I know where I am with that."

"Oh, you! That old tin caddy is over eighteen years old. I bought it before we got engaged; it's got pictures of the Coronation on it. No one uses souvenirs from the Coronation any more."

They sat outside a while and drank their tea in the fresh autumn sunshine; afterwards Dai went to potter in his greenhouse, and Eva went back into the kitchen. She noticed tiny black particles on the worktop, and wondered whether some thrips had flown in from the adjacent wheat field. When she realised that they were tea leaves leaking from her new dispenser, she quickly swept them away and put the Coronation caddy back in its usual place.

***

They decided to spend their sixteenth wedding anniversary with the family, and began their journey early in the morning. They reached Newport in good time, and Eva wondered if they could make a detour. "Do you think we've got time to call at Aberfan? I've always wanted to go and lay some flowers."

"Yes, if you like; I'll take the Merthyr Road via Risca. We can go up to the head of the Valleys, and drop down at Hirwaun for a change," replied Dai, wanting to go too.

Within the hour, the car was parked. Dai felt emotional. "There should be commemorations throughout Britain—not just in Wales."

"I agree there should, as a reminder that some people pay more than others in the name of commerce and industry. I've said it before, and I'll say it again; these coal seams are a curse on this area. It's too remote from Westminster, and easily overlooked. Come on let's go." Eva was almost in tears. All those people and the little children; it could so easily have been them.

They drove up the valley to the edge of the Beacons, and then west to Manddiogel. Nancy was waiting for them; they had telephoned from Aberfan telling her where they were, and that they wouldn't be long. "It will be five years ago next month since the Aberfan disaster— it's impossible to put into words the feelings of the folk around here," she said. "Come on, let's cheer up; there's a baby girl waiting to meet her great aunt and uncle."

Once the bags had been unpacked in the spare bedroom, the three of them walked across to the house. Several changes had been made: an Aga stood in place of the ancient range, and modern appliances had been added. Only the slate floor remained from the original kitchen. The front room was used daily, no longer the cold uncomfortable room that no one had liked in the past; now it was warm and cheerful, with a modern corner settee and a thick pile carpet fitted wall to wall. Lesley was curled up on the settee, with Beth sleeping by her side in a bassinet-style bed, which was kept in there for daytime sleeping.

"Come through," said Kath. "She's in here."

"Oh, isn't she gorgeous! How are you getting on?" Eva asked Lesley; she replied that she was feeling better each day, and that Mum was showing her what to do. Kath told them how much they were enjoying having a baby in the house again, and that the head master ensured she got all the information she needed to continue her studies at home.

"Mam's enjoying herself, not only with Beth, but with Lesley and her lessons; her teacher training all those years ago has been put to good use."

Next day, after chapel, Dai and Eva went to Mary's house for Sunday dinner. "We've been looking forward to you coming; isn't the new baby beautiful?" said Mary, as she took them into the lounge.

"She is gorgeous. I love the things you've made for her," replied Eva.

Em was making a fuss of Dai, and said excitedly, "Ethel and Peter are joining us for dinner, they'll be here in a minute." They arrived just at that moment. Peter produced a bottle of sweet sherry and a box of After Eight Mints. "Thank you very much, shall we have a sherry now?" asked Mary, giving Ethel a knowing look, as Em quickly went to fetch the sherry glasses from the sideboard.

Dai looked in astonishment as his mother confidently arranged the glasses. Mary laughed and explained. "She loves a glass of sherry on a Sunday before dinner, she got the taste for cream sherry a couple of Christmases ago. For a joke, Peter gave her a glass of sweet wine with her Christmas dinner last year, but she didn't like it."

After dinner, when everyone else was dozing in the front room, Eva and Ethel tidied the kitchen. "How's things then, Eth, have you got your house the way you want it yet?" asked Eva.

"I must admit I didn't want move into Pete's mam's house, but he inherited it so there wasn't much choice. We've done all can with it, and made it nice inside, but at the end of the day it's a cheaply built, terraced house overlooking the pit and the lorry depot. We want to sell it eventually; Pete thinks it'll make a decent deposit for one of those 1920s semis up near the park. We shouldn't have any trouble getting a mortgage, because we think the building society will consider some of my wages as well."

"That's a good idea; you'll be a bit nearer the workshop and on the better side of the village." Eva could imagine Ethel in one of those houses; she had been inside one once. It had three bedrooms, a tiny bathroom and kitchen downstairs, and an attractive living room with a bay window. There was a very small garden at the front, and a decent-sized one at the back with enough room for a greenhouse and shed. All things considered, it was a very nice house.

Ethel checked that they were out of earshot, and said, confidentially, "Don't say anything to Mam, but I'm worried about Mary; she's been having some awful headaches at work, she's not able to do anything until they pass. One day I had to close the shop early."

"You mean like a migraine? Does she wear glasses for close work?"

"Yes, she wears glasses when she's sewing or doing the books. It doesn't seem like a migraine to me, there's no bright lights or anything like that. She takes codeine tablets, but I think she needs to see the doctor."

"She ought to go; perhaps she needs a bit of persuasion."

"I'll keep trying. Let's join the others now, or they'll be wondering what we're up to."

Later in the afternoon, they left Mary's house and returned to Nancy's bungalow, to get ready for their evening drive back to Thornby.

***

On Remembrance Sunday, Peter telephoned to say that Mary was in hospital. "She's very poorly, Dai, she's had a stroke; she's having more tests tomorrow, and they're doing all they can, but it doesn't look good."

Dai put the receiver back on its cradle and told Eva, "Do you want to go to see her next weekend?" she asked.

"I think we should. Let's see how she is later in the week."

Early the following morning, they received another call from Peter. "It's bad news, I'm afraid, Mary died during the night, that first stroke did a lot of damage, and the second one was too much for her; I'm very sorry, Dai."

They did return to Wales, but not for a hospital visit; it was for Mary's funeral. Mary, the family's linchpin, supporter, and everyone's loyal friend, was gone.

After the funeral, Ethel and her brothers discussed Mam's future. Mary had left Ethel the tailoring business and the shop; the house went to Mam for the duration of her life, after which it was to be sold and the proceeds shared between the brothers. Everyone was concerned for Mam, because she was in her seventies and becoming frail; she would never cope with the house on her own.

Ethel and Peter had foreseen this issue, and had made a suggestion: they had intended to sell the house inherited from his mother, and to buy one of their choosing. They suggested that they sell their house as planned, and move in with Mam for as long as necessary. Dai and his brothers agreed with that idea instantly; it made sense, and got them off the hook as far as looking after Mam was concerned.

Ethel started worrying about the business, because knew she lacked Mary's skill and confidence to run it successfully. Peter said he would help with the accounts, but that was hardly running it— and, in any case, he had his own job to do. This worry carried on until two weeks before Christmas. On Wednesday half-day closing, Nancy had been to a coffee morning in the village hall with some women from the village; after the meeting she had a few minutes to get the red ribbon she need to make some bows for the Christmas tree. She hurried down the street to Ethel's shop before it closed.

Ethel was serving a customer, so Nancy looked around while she waited; when the customer left she went to the counter with a reel of ribbon. Ethel showed relief to see her. Nancy noticed instantly, and asked after her mother. Ethel told her that she wasn't doing very well; the light had gone out of her since Mary had died, and that even Peter couldn't cheer her.

"It's still early days. What about you? How are you coping with it all?" asked Nancy.

Ethel's eyes filled with tears; a moment later she was crying. "Stay with me Nancy, please don't go yet." Nancy looked at the clock on the wall; it was almost time to close for the rest of the day. She went to the door, and indicated that she was going to turn the sign round to 'Closed'. Ethel nodded. Nancy locked the door, and said, "Let's go through to the back; I'll make us some tea and you can tell me what's troubling you."

Ethel wiped her eyes, and said, "Everything's gone wrong since Mary died. We're trying to settle in with Mam, and yet she's still in a world of her own. Our house is up for sale, it's not going to sell now with Christmas just two weeks away, is it? And I'm not coping with this business; it's too much of a worry for me."

"If I remember rightly, you were going to put your house on the market next spring, weren't you?" Ethel nodded. "You've nothing to lose in that case. You never know—a buyer might come along in the new year. Don't you concern yourself with the house; let Peter deal with it. Now, what's the problem with the business?"

Ethel described the tailoring and soft furnishings operation in the workshop upstairs, and how Mary had run the shop. "Mary built all this over the years, and she understood the bones of it. I like the shop part, but the workshop is too pressurised, and I can't meet the deadlines. I should employ a seamstress, but I don't want to be an employer."

"I can't see Mary leaving you something she thought would be a burden; I think she intended you to do whatever you want with it." Nancy thought she might have a solution. "What do you and Peter intend to do in the long term?"

"We *were* hoping to buy a house near the park until all this happened. Now, I don't know."

"Have you considered closing down the workshop, and using some of the money from the sale of your house to turn it into a modern flat for you both later? I think you would cope with the shop, and I'm sure Peter would help you with the accounts until you got the hang of it. You could streamline your stock and sell only the faster-selling items of haberdashery, perhaps with some wool and knitting patterns, too. You could make some small items of soft furnishings, and sell them in the shop, if you want to. If you cut down on your stock holding, you might find that you've created space for a couple of tables and chairs where you could serve tea and cake. There's nowhere in the village to get a cup of tea or coffee, is there?"

"I'm sure Pete would be very happy with a flat; he hates gardening, and he wants to watch the rugby at the weekend. I can imagine us living in a nice modern home above the shop and its tearoom; the idea is very appealing."

"It's just a thought."

"Thank you, Nancy," Ethel felt much better and cut the four yards of ribbon. "For you, with my compliments."

Chapter Seventeen
1973

The previous year had ended badly. Five days before Christmas, Dai's mother died; she had diminished during the two years since Mary's death. Dai and Eva hadn't planned to go home for Christmas, but with Em's funeral taking place on the Thursday between Christmas and New Year, they decided to go this time, and stay for New Year.

Peter and Ethel were quiet, and wanted to be on their own, although Ethel was feeling brighter and more optimistic than she had in a long while. "This is a new beginning for us, isn't it Pete? The flat's ready, and our Sam can get on with selling the house now; we can move out whenever we like, can't we?"

"Yes, but I know Sam would like us to stay on here until it's sold. He thinks it'll go very quickly, because some houses have sold before they've been advertised," he replied.

He was right; by the end of January, Mary's house was sold, subject to contract, which meant that Peter and Ethel could move out in April, if everything went to plan.

Eva was shopping in town with a friend when Kath's letter arrived. Dai made himself a mug of coffee and settled down to read:

Gorse Wen Farm,
Manddiogel,
Glamorgan.
CF44 6JF

3rd, February 1973.

Dear Eva and Dai,

That's January out of the way for another year, thank goodness! There's some early signs of spring already; I think the mass of snowdrops in Copse Lane will be magnificent again. I wonder if anyone ever told you the story of those snowdrops? In case no one did, I'll tell you: that fabulous show which gets better by the year is down to just one man, Alf Evans, the postman. When he returned to the village after the war, he used to take a few bulbs in his pocket when he was delivering the post. He pushed them into the soft earth in the bank as he walked along the lane – today, his legacy is there for everyone's enjoyment.

I know you miss our early springs; the primroses in the woods will soon be in flower, and there are a few daffodils getting ready to open. It's starting to look very pretty. The birds are singing away, and there's the usual dollops of frog spawn in the ponds.

Mam's made a suggestion. She thinks it would be nice if we had a get-together in the summer, to celebrate this year's milestone birthdays. There's quite a few: your fortieths, Glynn's fiftieth, Sally will be twenty-one, and Lesley eighteen, Ginny will be fifty this year too, it would be nice to include her as well. Mam's hoping Glynn marries her soon, because she's got her eye on the bothy; she said if she moved in there, they could have the bungalow. I would like that, because I could nip through the adjoining door in the utility room, and it would save me going across the yard, especially in bad weather.

I saw Bob and Madge Lewis the other day; they've just come back from New Zealand. They went with their Michael and his wife Susan; they had a fabulous time. They said Barbara and John's farm was enormous. *They all ride horses, even Barbara. They've got an old Shetland pony; I think the children learned to ride on him. He's little Patrick's pony now. Of course, he's too young to ride it properly, but he's finding his balance very well.*

They were very taken with Barbara's little woollen mill; it makes a tidy profit too. She could expand, but she doesn't want to; she says it won't be a hobby if it gets too big. Some hobby! I think I've got a hobby baking and making crafts for the W. I.!

Anyway, if you fancy celebrating all the birthdays in the summer, let me know when you can come, and we'll get it organised.

Take care, and I'll give you a quick ring at the weekend.

Love, Kath xx

Dai read Kath's letter again; he knew that Eva would want to go home for their summer holiday this year because she wouldn't want to miss the party. He also knew that she would like to go to New Zealand and see Barbara, but that would cost a great deal of money, and he wouldn't want to go all that way for less than three weeks. He decided to look into it, and to see whether they could go the following winter, or perhaps the year after that.

When Eva read the letter, she suggested going home for two weeks in July. "How exciting! I bet Kath will push the boat out—any excuse!"

"I've been wondering if you'd like to go to New Zealand next year and visit Barbara," said Dai.

"I'd love to! I think it might be better if we went during the winter. If we went in January the year after, we wouldn't have any problems with our holiday entitlement, would we?"

"No, that's a good idea. If we went next January, we'd only be able to go home for one week in July wouldn't we? When Kath rings, let's tell her we'd like to stay for two weeks if Mam can cope with us for that long. If she thinks it would be a bit too much for her, we could go to Pembrokeshire for a few days."

At the beginning of July, Dai was promoted to Training and Development Manager; during his thirteen years with the company he had proven himself a competent engineer and a good trainer. In future, he was going to be responsible for all trainees, and the further development of established employees; it was agreed he would start his new role at the beginning of August, after his holiday.

***

Ethel and Peter had been living in the flat for ten weeks; all the old sash windows were replaced with double glazed aluminium ones. The workshop was now the living area with a new stone fireplace and enough room for dining and relaxing, and the kitchen was slick and modern, with cream units and a tiled worktop. The old stockroom was replaced by two bedrooms and a pretty bathroom, with a primrose suite and shower.

"I can't remember what it was like before Mary turned it into the workshop," said Dai to Ethel. "Where did I sleep when Dad was ill, and you stayed with Mam? I can't get my bearings at all."

"That's because it's the other way round; the bedrooms were on the front, and the sitting room and kitchen area were in one room at the back," she replied.

"I remember now; what a transformation! It's so light and bright. Are you pleased you decided not to buy a house after all?"

"Definitely. This is so easy to look after; when Peter isn't at work we have time to do as we please, and I feel much safer here when he's on nights. Before you go, we'll show you what we've done with the shop; you won't recognise that either." Ethel was happy, she was married to a cheerful, hardworking man who adored her, he had turned this gloomy old building into a pleasant place for her to live and work.

"Oh this is quite charming," said Eva, casting an admiring glance around the shop. Neat displays of haberdashery and a small counter with a till were on one side of the shop; on the other was the tea and coffee area, furnished with Mary's dresser and matching dining table and six chairs. Also, there was an old Pembroke table and four chairs, which had once belonged to Peter's mother. The front window was a Georgian bow with some panes featured in bottle-glass; hanging from a brass track on the lower third of the window was a pretty net curtain. The deep windowsill displayed bric-a-brac with price tags. Dotted all around the room were small items of interest, some for sale, others for decoration. It looked like the kind of shop you'd find in an upmarket town.

"I can cope with this," said Ethel confidently. "I keep minimum levels of stock, and if someone wants an item I haven't got, I can usually get it for them within a few days. The tea and cakes are popular; in fact, they're more profitable than the haberdashery—as long as I don't make my customers too comfortable, and they stay all morning with one drink!"

Peter said, "I'd like to knock through to the back of the shop and develop the café. I reckon there's more that can be done with this place."

Dai's thoughts were of Mary when they left—her influence over Ethel and him, the way she had dealt with Dad when he was being difficult, and the love and support she had given to Mam after he died—oh, how he did miss her!

***

It was the third Saturday morning in July, half way through Dai and Eva's holiday, and the day of the party. They had spent the previous week catching up with old friends and visiting their favourite places. Lately, the weather had been disappointing, with little sunshine, but today was going to be glorious; the sky was baby-blue, with a few wispy clouds, and it was going to be hot.

Kath and Nancy were preparing the food, and Eva was laying the table for the buffet. The men took themselves out of the way with the dogs; they walked along the path in the meadow that Glynn had cut with the tractor and flail. What a long-lost sight this was for Dai: the meadow on both sides of the path was stuffed with countless different grasses, all in seed now and wafting idly in the breeze. Meadowsweet grew almost up to his waist; the fragrance from this beautiful plant was intoxicating, and knapweed's pretty purple heads competed with golden buttercups to be the boldest colour among the spectacle. Insects, dozens of different species, buzzed and fluttered from plant to plant; he had not seen a field this alive for years, certainly not since he had left Wales. He passed comment.

"Don't you have wild flower meadows in Leicestershire?" enquired Glynn.

"Not like they used to, apparently; they grow a lot of cereal crops and spray them to kill the pests."
"When they spray, the wild flowers die too; even those that grow in hedgerows have suffered, because a lot of the hedges have been ripped out to make way for larger fields. That one next to us has either rape or wheat in it. The only insects I've ever seen coming from there are what they call thrips; tiny black flies, and a damn nuisance they are too. They get everywhere, even in the

picture frames. An old boy, who's lived in the village all his life, says he can remember when that field was full of buttercups and cowslips, and the lanes full of primroses, just like they are here. The only wild flowers I've seen in the lanes are dandelions and an occasional poppy."

They crossed the ford, and walked along the river bank, past the colliery and up the hill toward the village, until they reached the cemetery. If it hadn't been for the dogs, they might have gone in; but to take four dogs in there wasn't seemly, so they continued toward the village.

As they approached the Collier's Arms, Dai asked if they wanted a swift half; they ordered a pint each and sat in the garden with the dogs. They discussed the local rugby team at length, as well as the new Sony factory in Bridgend, the troubles in Northern Ireland, and countless other topics. Another round of drinks took them to more personal things, about Glynn mainly, but not before Dai told them about his new job as Training and Development Manager. "There's posh," said Glynn. "Do you get an office with your name on the door?"

Dai laughed. "Not quite, there's a desk in the corner of the training room with my name on."

"Good for you. It's well deserved, moving away as you did; not many of us would have had the guts, especially with a wife as settled as Eva was," said Tom.

"Come on then, Glynn, spill the beans. What's happening with you and Ginny?" asked Dai.

Glynn nodded, "We're going to get married; she's ready now the boys are grown and have moved out, and she knows she won't get a slap from me if my dinner isn't ready or if she comes home ten minutes late."

"Had it pretty rough, did she?"

"Yes. He wasn't a violent man in public, but he did hit her when he lost his temper at home. There's something about Ginny that makes her a target for bullies; I saw it when we were at school. I always felt a need to protect her, but when she was old enough to start dating, Jim Faulks came along, got her pregnant and that was me out of it. I've bided my time since he was killed, and now I'm going to bring her home, to live with us on the farm."

"We all want her there," said Tom. "You know what Kath's like; she'll soon have her settled. Mam's made it clear she wants the bothy, which means Glynn and Ginny can have the bungalow. A good outcome all round, wouldn't you say?"

"Indeed, I'm very pleased for you," said Dai.

The three men and the dogs continued their walk through the village, along the footpath at the back of the post office, and down the hill past Felin Fach; they crossed over the leat, and arrived at the farm.

"Ah, there you are! Just in time to move the garden furniture over here, please," said Kath, as soon as they entered the yard. It was such a beautiful day; everyone would want to be outside on a day like this. They had plenty of seats and benches scattered around the place; all she needed was a strong person to move them closer to the house.

Paul arrived just after Glynn left to fetch Ginny. He was tired after having travelled from Guildford all morning. "The traffic was horrendous; everyone seems to be heading for the West Country. It's taken me twice as long as normal to get here."

"Never mind, at least you've been able to come; go upstairs and freshen up, while Dad gets you a drink." She had been waiting anxiously; he usually arrived earlier than this on a Saturday. Last time he had come home, he had brought unwelcome news, as far as she was concerned, because the company he worked for had a contract in Saudi Arabia. Paul was one of a small team of civil engineers being sent there for two years, and this was going to be his last trip home for quite some time.

Glynn arrived with Ginny, and everyone gathered in the sunshine; champagne corks popped, and the party began. Lesley fetched a cushion for Nancy. "Here you are, Granny, this'll be more comfortable for you."

"Thank you, cariad." *She's just like Kath, thoughtful and caring; not at all like Sally, unless you've got four legs!* She watched everyone while sipping her champagne: there was Glynn, fussing over the love of his life, while she laughed at the things he said and looked at him with such loving eyes—she was pleased he'd won her over in the end. Tom and Kath were chatting with Paul, their eldest, who was about to work overseas for two years; Sally, whose twenty-first birthday was a few days previously, her entire life dedicated to horses; and young Lesley, with her little daughter Beth. She wished more than anything that, one day, Lesley would meet someone nice and have more children. And there was Eva and Dai; she, the private secretary to the most senior partner in the law firm, and he newly promoted into the management team of that huge engineering company in England.

She couldn't be more proud of her family; she thought of Stan, and how sad it was that he hadn't lived to see all this; a tear welled, and she wiped it away quickly.

"Nana, look!" It was Beth showing her the fluffy camel which Paul had bought her. "Uncle Paul says he'll be riding one of these in the desert." Nancy glanced at her grandson; he shrugged, and gave her a wink.

The party continued outside, until the sun went down, and it started to get chilly. "What a perfect day; I'm so pleased everyone could make it. Let's do it again, next time Paul comes home," said Nancy.

The weather remained sunny and mainly dry for the rest of the week. Dai and Eva took Nancy and Beth on day trips to the Gower, and the seaside villages in Carmarthenshire. On Saturday morning, they returned to Leicester.

***

Dai started his new job on the following Monday. His predecessor called in briefly during the morning to hand over the on-going issues. Later, while he was sorting out the files in his desk, the staff manageress appeared in the doorway. "Hello, Dai, had nice holiday? How are you getting on?" Before he could answer, she continued. "There's a new mechanic starting tomorrow; he'll need a fire-tour, please. Does ten o'clock suit you?" He told her it did; she thanked him and breezed off.

Next day, at ten o'clock sharp, the new mechanic entered the training room; Dai shook his hand and asked him to sit down. He knew that the man's name was Ron Hamilton, but nothing else. Ron told Dai about his past work experiences, and gave a brief summary of his life. "I am Jamaican; I was seven when I arrived in Birmingham with my parents and two sisters in 1955. When I was twenty-two, I got married and moved to Leicester, because my wife's family live here."

Dai showed him where his locker and the canteen were and gave him the fire-tour; afterwards, he took him to his place of work and introduced him to his foreman.

During September, Eva received a letter from Barbara:

Killorglin,
Hawsker,
Christchurch,
N. Z.

12th, September 1973

Dear Eva,

 Thank you very much for the lovely photographs of the party; seeing you all again at the farm made me homesick. It's hard to think of Glynn being fifty. I'm ever so pleased he's going to marry Ginny; if only he'd been quicker off the mark all those years ago! Never mind, better now than never.

 I'm sorry to say my fortieth birthday wasn't as nice as yours, because I found out that John's been having an affair. It was such a bolt out of the blue; I had no idea. One of my friends saw them together; she challenged him until he admitted it. She told him that if he didn't tell me, she would, so, with an ultimatum hanging over him, he told me.

 We're in an awful mess. He's had to make a choice, and he's chosen me, but the fact is he had no choice. This is his home; his business and his children are here. I don't know quite where I sit among all that.

 His mam and sisters have come down on my side, and they are being truly awful to him. His sisters won't speak to him, and his mother's been very hurtful. His dad says he's been a bloody fool, and although he supports me, he's much kinder to him than everyone else is.

 At times I actually feel a bit sorry for him; he's beating himself up and he looks terrible. He says he loves me, and he doesn't know what came over him. I do: this woman is everything I'm not. She's an accountant at the firm dealing with the farm's taxes. She's Dutch and about twenty-five years of age, she's tall, slim and very elegant. She wears expensive suits and high heeled shoes most of the time, whereas I wear scruffy trousers and riding boots or wellies. I'm told she's a very nice person, although how a very nice person can do this to a woman with four children is beyond me.

I don't think it went on for long. He says he didn't love her; he says it was just 'fun', but now he's feeling very ashamed, and begging me to forgive him. I don't know if I can; I feel as though I'm the mother of a naughty child who expects to be scolded, and then a cuddle will make everything right again. Leaving him isn't an option, so it's in everyone's interest for me to forgive him and move on.

I've never felt so far from home, and, for the first time, I've regretted coming here. John's family have been wonderful, but they are his family, not mine. What I would give to see someone from Wales just now—anyone.

I think I'll leave it there for now; please don't tell Mam and Dad, and don't worry about me, I'll be okay.

With my love,
Barbara xx

Chapter Eighteen

A comfortable acquaintanceship had developed between Dai and Ron since the latter joined the company two years previously; when there was a change in him, Dai quickly noticed. He wondered why he was sitting on his own in the canteen, instead of joining the other men, sharing jokes and bantering as he used to.

On his way to work one morning, Dai saw him waiting at a bus stop. He stopped and offered him a lift, which he accepted. "My car's having a new exhaust fitted; it almost fell off yesterday!" Ron explained. They chatted about trivial things, until he confided. "My marriage is in trouble. My wife Connie is a teacher, and she's having problems in the classroom. She's not strong enough to control the pupils; they are rude and undisciplined, and it's not unusual for her to get verbal abuse, especially from some of the white kids. She's decided to leave England and join a team of overseas workers who teach in Tanzania. I would like us to start a family, but she says she doesn't want a child of her own because there's thousands over there needing help. She seems as though she has a calling to go."

"Is going with her an option; are there jobs out there for skilled mechanics?" asked Dai, recalling his past dilemma.

"No, it's not an option, at least not for me. I couldn't work in Africa. I'll stay here and see what happens when she's been there a while. We get on really well, and I thought we were happy together; she insists we are, but it's not enough."

***

After many months of planning, Dai and Eva were ready to go on their holiday to New Zealand. Ron offered to take them to Heathrow Airport, because he had driven there several times before and was familiar with the route. The journey was easy enough, with the usual congestion on Bath Road, which he allowed for; he took them to Departures, and said that he would be waiting for them in Arrivals in three weeks' time.

Air New Zealand announced the flight's departure, and an hour later they were airborne, heading for Hong Kong; after a break of several hours, the flight continued to Christchurch. The aircraft landed in the early evening; the sun was still shining, and it was twenty-one degrees, not the kind of January evening they were accustomed to.

From the observation deck, John and Barbara watched a DC10 land and taxi to its port. They looked at the information board, and saw the Heathrow flight was displayed as 'Landed'. They made their way to Arrivals, and waited among the dozens of other excited people for their friends to appear.

Eva spotted Barbara waving and laughing, "There they are, look; they've seen us!" she exclaimed. They threaded their way through the crowd until they were together; the old friends kissed and hugged, and cried a little, just like everyone else with their family and friends.

John took charge of the baggage, and led the way to his six-seater pick up in the car park. It was a two-tone blue monster with two huge leather bench seats, and a lot of space for carriage. Dai was awestruck. "My word, I've driven smaller lorries than this! I wouldn't like to feed it!"

"It's greedy; it does about twelve to the gallon on a good trip. It's useful, though, because we can get the kids and all the clobber in; you must try it out while you're here, and see what you think."

When the baggage and passengers were on board, John started the engine, and drove out of the car park on to the dual carriageway, in the direction of Hawsker. Ninety minutes later, he turned into the entrance of Killorglin, and drove for several hundreds of yards, past gently sloping pasture and fenced paddocks.

On the right hand side of the drive was a large house that looked as though it might have been built in the 1930s, and stylishly altered several times since. John told them that this was the family home, where his parents lived. About a hundred yards farther on was a modern ranch, which had been extended on both sides. "This is our house—do you see that building over there?" asked Barbara, pointing to a barn-like structure with a water wheel attached to the side. "That's my mill, just wait until you see it! You'll think you're back in Manddiogel!"

John parked outside the ranch and unloaded the luggage; a tall robust woman in her mid sixties opened the front door. She greeted them, and said she was John's mother. Four curious young people appeared from behind her – they were Barbara's children.

A strange feeling overcame Eva; these were her best friend's children, and she yet had never seen them. Until twenty years ago, she had known everything about Barbara there was to know; now she felt she knew very little.

Barbara introduced the children starting with the eldest, "This is Jonathan; this is Heather; and these two are Rachael and Patrick."

Eva acknowledged each in turn, and observed them as they went inside: Jonathan was tall and impressive-looking, with a pleasant demeanour. Heather, at fifteen, was tall and fair; she resembled the grandmother standing beside her. It made Eva wonder about the nationality of this grandmother's ancestors. Rachael was a short pretty girl with mousy hair; she favoured the Lewis side of the family, not as dark-haired as Barbara, but she definitely saw a likeness with Madge. And Patrick? Anyone's guess. He was certainly going to be tall like his father and elder brother; a likeable, cheeky-looking imp who would, no doubt, be good fun to be with during the next three weeks.

Maggie, Barbara's mother-in-law, noticed how tired Dai and Eva were; she excused herself, saying she was looking forward to getting to know them, and she would meet them again when they were rested and settled.

Next morning, Eva woke after a deep sleep. She wondered where she was—until she recalled that she was in Barbara's home. Not wanting to miss a moment, she got up, and drew back the curtains. "Just look at this, Dai," she said, opening the window wider. Their room had a double aspect; from the side window, she saw Barbara's mill. Two cars were parked alongside the river nearby; she assumed they belonged to the workers. The other window overlooked the wide gravel driveway and the turning circle at the front of the house; on each side of the drive were several well-kept paddocks, with smart ranch fencing. John's parents' house was on the left of the vista; the white shutters and the huge front porch with comfortable seating gave it a colonial look.

Dai got out of bed, and joined Eva at the window, "Very impressive, isn't it? I had no idea she was living like this."

"Me neither, she's been very discreet, hasn't she?"

"No wonder she decided to stay," he remarked good-naturedly.

"Shush," she laughed, digging him in the ribs.

There was a knock on their bedroom door; it was Barbara, holding a mug in each hand. "Good morning! I've brought you some tea. Did you sleep well?"

"We did, thank you. That was quite a journey; it knocked us out," said Eva. "What a fabulous place this is! It's not at all as I imagined; I thought it would be like those pictures of the Outback in Australia, all barren and dried up."

Barbara sat on the bed, "Oh no, it's not like that at all; in fact, you'll see similarities with Wales. There's a long range of alps which runs the length of the island, and there's a lot of lakes; although we do get less rain and more sun here—but when it shines on the snow-capped mountains, it's absolutely breathtaking."

"I can't wait to see everything; I know you've told me about it in your letters, but I didn't think for one moment it would be like this," enthused Eva.

Barbara smiled, and said, "I'll leave you both to get ready. Take your time; when you come down, we'll have a nice big breakfast and a tour of the place." She left them to finish their tea and unpack their cases.

They wondered whether this room was part of the recent extension, because it was substantial; it had a private bathroom, which made it more like a suite. "I suppose this is where her mam and dad, or perhaps Michael and Susan, slept when they came; I bet they're imagining us here, and wondering what we're doing," Eva commented.

After they showered and dressed, they went downstairs into the lounge where Barbara was waiting, "John won't be long; he's gone to have a word with the foreman. Come and talk to me in the kitchen while I make us some breakfast. I hope you don't mind; John and the children have had theirs, it's always an early start here, just like on the farms back home."

"No, that's all right; we'll be up early from tomorrow. We don't want to miss a thing," replied Dai.

The three of them chatted over breakfast. Barbara told them more about John's family, and they brought her up to date with news from Manddiogel and told her about their life in England.

Barbara was giving them a tour of the house when John joined them; he explained that his parents had built the original house for him when he returned with Barbara. When the babies started to arrive, a wing with two more bedrooms was added. After Patrick's arrival five years ago, a matching wing was added to the other side of the house. The interior was remodelled, to create two guest suites, five bedrooms with en suites, and a bathroom. There was an enormous lounge downstairs, a huge dining kitchen with an adjacent laundry and utility room, a playroom, and an office.

Dai and Eva were enthralled. They had never stayed in such a grand building, and yet there was an air of modesty about the place. This house was a home; the pictures on the walls were prints. There were no expensive ornaments to be concerned about if the children were boisterous; a cat was asleep on an easy chair, and a there was a dog basket in the kitchen. It was a lovely home with a nice atmosphere—they felt they could stay forever.

They went to see the outbuildings next; Rachael and Patrick were playing in the stable block, and Heather was cleaning tack. It brought to mind Sally and her ponies at Gorse Wen Farm. Everything here was bigger and newer, but the running of the farm and the lives of the people were similar.

John was showing Dai the barns and machinery. It looked as though they were going to be a while yet. Barbara was anxious for Eva to see her mill. "Join us at the mill when you've finished here, John; keep Patrick with you please, I don't want him near the machines while I'm speaking to Eva."

The two women walked along the footpath leading from the barns to the mill. As they approached, Barbara proudly proclaimed, "Here it is, Manddiogel Mill."

Eva gazed at the building before her: it was roughly the size of the Bethesda Chapel, built of local stone with a slate roof. Attached to the riverside wall was a waterwheel, which was turning. It gave the impression of a Welsh woollen mill in the 1800s, quaint and out of place, and yet quite charming, like a picture in a child's story book. "It isn't water-powered, surely?" she queried.

"Not entirely; the wheel provides some power, especially in the winter when the river flows faster, but there's a supporting generator and mains power as well. Some of the machines are manual. There's a treadle spinning wheel; it's very popular with the women, because they think it keeps their legs in shape; come on I'll show you."

Eva remembered going to see Barbara at work when they had first left school; the noise had been deafening, and everywhere had been coated with fluff from the wool. Here, where possible, buffers had been fixed inside the machinery to muffle the clatter of metal on metal, and modern extractor fans kept the air almost free of particles.

"I keep the fleeces in one of the barns we've just left; they're filthy things, so we don't bring them over until we're ready to use them. There's a variety of breeds, and depending where they graze, their wool quality varies. I choose the best and give John's dad the current price, minus twenty per cent discount."

She showed Eva the carding machine located behind a screen. "We card by machine, because it's an unpleasant job to do by hand; it's noisy, too, that's why it's behind the screen." She took Eva to the spinning wheels next. "This is the treadle; it's very old as you can see, but with a good operator, it's almost as fast as the power driven one." She moved to the next section. "These are the dye vats; the colours are pastel, because they're more suitable for what we produce." Finally they entered a separate room; a machine filled it. "This monster is the loom. I'm fortunate to have this, because it's British. John's dad got it for me at an auction; apparently it was brought here decades ago. My goodness, it can fly; you'll be able to see it in action in a few minutes."

"Do you sell the cloth as it leaves the loom, like the mill at home does?" asked Eva.

"Yes, and I'll weave tweed if I'm asked, but my main manufacture is blankets. Sometimes, if John has some fleeces that aren't good enough to sell, he'll give them to me and we make them into felt blankets for horses."

"I was surprised when you said you were starting a mill; I thought you might have had enough of that kind of work," Eva remarked.

"The idea evolved; when I first arrived, John's dad was curious about the Manddiogel mill. It sparked something in his mind; all his life he had produced wool on a large scale and sold the fleeces to the factory mills. As John became more involved with running the farm, his dad got interested in processing on a small scale. I had the practical experience, and before we knew it, we'd built a mill in our imaginations—and here we are, almost twenty years later, with a profitable little business. It's a hobby, really. John's dad put the money up and got the mill built; I went with him to choose the machinery, and he paid for it. He doesn't get involved with running it, but he loves to see it working, and will often come just for the pleasure of being here."

"How many people do you employ?" asked Eva.

"There's five part-timers, plus one outdoor worker. Two of them are retired farm labourers; they work the loom, the carding machine, and see to the porterage. Three women do the spinning, bleaching and dying, and the outdoor worker binds the edges of the blankets. If we get behind with the orders, I'll pitch in; John's dad will operate the carder if we're really stuck; and there's a couple of farm workers' wives who will come and lend a hand if necessary. We could update and be more automated, but it wouldn't be a hobby any more, so we won't do that. The machines are old, and the loom is limited, but it all works perfectly well, and if they do break down they're easy to fix."

"I think it's fascinating; it must be lovely to have a hobby that gives a cash return too," said Eva. "I don't think we'll be seeing much of Dai once he gets in here; I think he'll be applying for a job as the mechanic!"

Eva met the workers; the carding machine was not operating, because a lot of wool had been prepared for the spinners the day before. Both wheels were spinning, and a pile of skeins was on the floor ready to be taken to the vats; Eva watched the weaver put the loom in motion, and continue from where he left off the day before.

John, Dai and the two children joined them, but Eva wanted to speak to Barbara alone. "Let's have a stroll along the river bank while they look at the machines," she suggested, anxious to know if Barbara was as happy and content as she appeared to be.

"We're all right now, Eva; it's behind us. It doesn't matter any more. We're not exactly love's young dream, but we are happy together, and that's all that matters."

"All couples change, Barbara, they either grow together or they grow apart; I'm pleased you were strong enough to ride it out, and are happy again."

Three fabulous weeks followed. John and Barbara took them to the lakes, and they spent two nights near the Aoraki/Mount Cook National Park; they met their friends, and more of John's relations, and played with the children. They were feeling quite settled by the time the holiday was over, and they were due to return home.

"Stay here, why go back? You'd both get good jobs," said Barbara, attempting to persuade them.

"It's too late for us, Barbara; if we had come to see you years ago we might have been tempted, but we couldn't do it now. You've been here twenty years and you have your children; before long, you'll have grandchildren. You saw an opportunity at the right time, and you took it."

Disappointed, yet understanding, Barbara said, "Come again if you can, won't you?"

"We'll come again, you can be sure of that."

Chapter Nineteen
1986

Dai and Eva planned to go to Wales for the Christmas holiday; they always visited the family at least once a year, but not usually at Christmas. They were going this year however, because Nancy was now eighty-five and very frail.

Eva switched off her word processor, wished those who were still there a Happy Christmas, and went to the car park where her VW Golf was parked. She was collecting Dai on her way home, because the factory closed at lunch time and he was having a Christmas drink with some friends from work in the pub across the road.

Next morning, Dai loaded his Volvo with presents and luggage, and, by eight o'clock, they were on their way. After some expected delays at the NEC, Monmouth, and Newport, they arrived at the farm late in the afternoon. They were staying in the farmhouse with Tom and Kath. Paul, his wife Marcia, and their two daughters Penny and Jess, were staying with Glynn and Ginny in the bungalow.

Eva said she would like to look after Nancy while they were there; Kath was happy with that, because it would give her a break, and more time to spend preparing for the festivities.

"Mam's very frail now, Eva; you'll see a big change in her since your last visit. Ginny does all her cleaning and laundry, and I see to everything else. She's no trouble, though." She opened the door to the adjoining bothy, and Eva stepped inside. The door to the lounge was slightly ajar. Through the gap, she saw Nancy dozing in her chair; there was a pretty tartan blanket over her lap. The stripes in the tartan perfectly matched her blue cardigan and slippers.

Kath gently touched Nancy's arm to rouse her. "Mam, look who's come to see you; it's Eva, she's come to spend Christmas with us." Nancy slowly lifted her head and looked first at Kath, then at Eva. Recognition gradually crept into her weary eyes. Eva noticed immediately that Nancy's once hazel eyes had lost their colour, and were now pale blue-grey; her hair was fine silver, and cut very short. Kath was right, there had been changes; nevertheless Eva thought she looked lovely, and extremely well cared for.

The following morning, Kath gave her Nancy's care routine. "I'll leave you to it; I'll be around here if you need me." An hour later, Eva joined Kath in the house. "Hi, how did you get on?" asked Kath.

"Awful! I was so clumsy, it took ages to get her washed and dressed; she actually got a bit irritable with me."

Kath smiled knowingly, "She does get tetchy sometimes; she's a bit like a child. They don't like being washed and dressed either. Shall I see to her tonight?"

"No, I'd like to do it."

"All right, do say if you change your mind."

Fourteen people were seated around the table in the farmhouse kitchen that evening. Kath prepared a simple meal: chicken in creamy sauce with rice for Nancy and Paul's daughters, and two large casseroles simmered on the Aga for everyone else. One contained chicken curry, and the other, chilli con carne. Chunks of homemade bread were in baskets at each end of the table; orange juice and bottles of white wine were in the fridge, and an opened bottle of red wine was on the worktop. Kath gave Nancy a small bowl of chicken and rice, and shared the rest between Penny and Jess. Ginny served either the curry or the chilli con carne to the others.

While they were eating, the conversation got around to the many changes in the area. "Did you notice the pit, or what's left of it?" asked Tom.

"We did," replied Dai. "We saw that the winding wheel tower was down and lying on its side, and some of the buildings are gone. Do you know what they are planning to do with it?"

"I think they'll clear the site and leave it—that's what they've done with other mines. I suppose they'll reduce the slag heap as much as possible, and leave it to grow over. No doubt it'll blend with the landscape eventually."

"The village is going to look quite different, isn't it?" commented Paul. "Much better without that monstrosity blotting the landscape."

Glynn agreed, "Oh without doubt; but the redundancies and the knock-on effect are a serious issue. Twenty years ago, when there were pit closures, there was work to be found elsewhere, but it's not like that now; that's why there's so much ill feeling towards the government."

"It's not only the pit that's closed; all the haulage has moved to Cardiff. The slaughter-house has shut down because it didn't meet the latest legislation, the number of animals passing through had reduced; therefore it was deemed not cost effective to make the necessary alterations," said Tom.

"What we need is new enterprise; those of us with an opportunity to diversify should do so," announced Sally. "Dad and I have been thinking about starting an equine business; the farm as it is at the moment struggles to make ends meet, and is physically demanding for Dad and Uncle Glynn these days."

"What have you got in mind?" asked Eva.

Sally explained that they were considering several options, based on what was happening elsewhere. "There's a lot of money being made, especially in England. Some people have bought properties in Wales to use as holiday homes; our idea is to make the farm attractive for activity holidays, or relaxing in a quiet location. If we convert some of the barns and out-buildings into self-catering accommodation, and perhaps provide Bed and Breakfast as well, some people might use us as a base for exploring the Brecon Beacons or the coast. We could provide livery, and maybe even start a riding school with trekking—perhaps boarding kennels and a cattery, too. There is so much scope; the possibilities are endless."

Eva could see that it was an exciting prospect for Sally. It would take a young person to have the confidence and the energy to do all this; she could also see how drastically the village would have to change in order to avoid becoming a victim of the changes that were hitting the area hard and fast. She spoke to Kath about it later. "Is it viable, do you think?"

"It is, if Tom and the girls have the drive and determination to do it. Paul's made some profit projections that are favourable. If we stay as we are, we'll struggle, because our pensions and the reduced income from the sheep won't be enough for us—and with the long term upkeep of the buildings and land, it looks as though we haven't much choice."

Who'd manage the farm in the future? Eva wondered inwardly. It looked likely to be Sally, with support from Lesley and Beth. There was no possibility of Paul's return, because he was settled in Marcia's home town in Surrey; all her family lived close by, and he had his career.

"We have to think about the girls and their future, because the farm is going to be short of men and young people; I thought there would be more grandchildren to run the farm, but Penny and Jess are out of the equation, which leaves only Beth. Fortunately, she takes after her Auntie Sally and her love of horses. When she's finished her education, she'll most likely work with her."

"It's quite a dilemma, isn't it?" said Eva. "All farms require a great deal of maintenance. I expect a lot of land is left to grow wild these days."

"Ours is; then the brambles take over and render it useless."

Christmas Day started as would any normal day, with the animals and other essential jobs attended to first. The women were concerned that dinner might not be over in time for the Queen's Speech, and debated whether to postpone it until afterwards. Penny and Jess were enthralled by the ponies, and insisted that they spend all day with them in the stables. There were tears from both when it was pointed out that they must eat their Christmas dinner at the table, and not in the stable with the ponies.

Dinner was served at one o'clock, and now, having seen the Queen on television, Nancy was dozing in the front room. Her mind drifted back over the years, until it settled on her first Christmas at the farm when she had been a young bride, sixty-four years ago. *Her father-in-law was sitting in the carver chair that later became Stan's; that was their only Christmas without children, because the following year Glynn was born.*

Her mind wandered on to 1939. *The first Christmas of the war and Eva's first with them; earlier in the month she lit eight candles, one a day, for Hanukkah. And then there was that sad Christmas, her first without Stan. Moving on five years, a new baby in the house again: it all came good in the end, look at that baby now, lovely Beth, a teenager with her whole life ahead of her. Glynn and Tom were concerned about the future of the farm, but there really was no need; the next generation would diversify and take it forward.*

Eva was reminiscing, too. She couldn't remember much about that first Christmas in Wales, only flashes of how strange it had all seemed to her as a Jewish child. She did remember later ones, when she was growing up: the school concerts, Midnight Masses, and missing Dad terribly after he died. She glanced across at Nancy; she seemed lost in her own thoughts. She watched Kath go to her, and ask if she would like to go to bed now. Nancy stirred and nodded. Eva joined Kath and helped take her through to the bothy and to bed.

Boxing Day was spent with Ethel and Peter in their flat, above what was now their tearoom and café. Peter had been made redundant when the haulier's depot closed; he had invested his redundancy money in shares, and, in two years' time, he would be able to claim his state and company pensions. In the mean time they lived off their savings and the income from the shop. "It's the best thing that could have happened to me," he told them. "Driving long distances and being away from home was taking its toll; now I help Ethel in the shop and don't need to worry about a thing."

"Have the recent closures affected the café?" asked Dai, mindful of the local redundancies.

"Yes, but in a positive way. We're busier than ever because a lot of our customers are visitors to the area, or people from outside the village who come to the new supermarket, or to visit the medical centre. The changes have gone in our favour."

"Have you heard about Tom and Sally's idea of turning the farm into an equestrian holiday centre?" asked Dai.

"We have, it's the talk of the village—and a damned good idea if you ask me. We need more of this kind of thing to bring money into the area. Of course there's the usual band of parochial old sods who don't want newcomers or visitors; I think they'd rather see the village sink into the abyss. Instead of moaning and making life difficult for others, they ought to get off their backsides and do something positive for once; they make me sick!"

Ethel laughed at Peter's frustration. "He gets quite passionate about the future of the village; I've told him he ought to join the Parish Council."

"I might just do that!"

When Christmas was over, Glynn asked Dai if they could stay a few days longer. "It seems a pity to go if you don't need to; stay and see the New Year in with us."

How thankful they were that they did! At the end of March, when Kath took Nancy a cup of tea, she thought at first that she was asleep in her chair—until she realised she wasn't sleeping at all. Tears filled her eyes as she went to tell the others that Nancy was with Stan and baby Elizabeth.

Chapter Twenty
2006

The years flew by with mixed sadness and joy; for some there were new beginnings, for others there were sad endings. The village went into mourning with the news of Gwen Hughes's passing; she died in a Cardiff nursing home, not far from where she had been born, ninety-one years previously. The village school erected a slate plaque with gold lettering, dedicated to her memory, in the foyer.

Tom died of respiratory failure in 2000. He had been suffering chest infections for several winters; during this one, he caught pneumonia and was unable to recover. Shortly afterwards, Glynn and Ginny decided to move into the bothy, and the vacant bungalow was turned into an additional holiday let.

Sally's equine business continued from strength to strength; a row of modern prefabricated stables was erected, and a training area replaced the chicken enclosure. There were no sheep; at first, the farm was eerily quiet without their bleating, and the distant fields were empty of the small white dots which had been scattered in them for almost two centuries.

Lesley's daughter Beth married the history teacher from the comprehensive school; they had two boys, and were living in one of the houses on the new development where the haulage depot used to be. A block of retirement maisonettes was built on the edge of the development. Peter and Ethel sold their flat and tearooms, and moved into one of them.

John and Barbara's family in New Zealand continued to increase; their four children had families of their own and there were many grandchildren. The only sadness they experienced was when John's parents died in the early 1990s.

Eva saw the postman walking up the path. When she heard the letter box snap shut, she went into the hall and picked up the two envelopes on the mat. One was from Wales, the other from New Zealand; she opened Kath's letter first:

Gorse Wen Farm,
Manddiogel,
Glamorgan
CF44 6JF

29th, August 2006

Dear Eva,

I know it's not long since we spoke on the telephone, but we always have so much to talk about, and I never remember to tell you everything, so today I thought I would put pen to paper and write you a letter for a change.

First of all, I know it's a long way to come, and I quite understand if you don't feel able, but next year I'm having a small party for my eightieth birthday, just the family and a few friends, and I would love you both to come. The girls are arranging it, so I won't need to do a thing; in fact I don't do much at all these days. Lesley says it's time for me to be a lady of leisure!

I'm grateful that Glynn and Ginny moved into the bothy; it's nice to have someone my own age around. I would have been lonely these past six years since Tom died, if it hadn't been for them. The girls are very good to the three of us, but they are terribly busy, and don't have time to just 'be' with us. There's a family on holiday in the bungalow at the moment; there aren't many weeks it stands empty. The same goes for the barns; there's usually someone in them, even it's only for the weekend.

Sally and Lesley have got the business down to a fine art. Sally sees to the horses and ponies, the lessons and the trekking, and Lesley manages the accounts and the holiday accommodation. Beth and her family have settled in their new house in the village; when the boys are at school, she comes and helps Lesley. Recently, she's been able to help clean the barns and change the linen on Saturday mornings. Her husband is quite happy to look after the boys as long as she's back in time for him to go to the rugby match in the afternoon.

There's going to be more new houses built in the village, this time on the site of the old slaughter house. It'll be an improvement, because the old building has been falling down for twenty years. It was ugly enough when it was in use, so you can imagine what it looks like now, with all the windows smashed and weeds growing through the concrete. Apart from that eyesore, the village is looking quite tidy. Ethel's tearooms has changed hands again. It's been given a new name this time; they've called it the Honey Pot. It's quite quirky; even the tablecloths and napkins have honey bees printed on them. I saw Ethel the other day; she said that they're quite comfortable and happy in their little maisonette. Peter struggles with his walking, but, apart from that, he's okay.

Do you remember where the florist's shop was before the supermarket put her out of business? Well, it's a dentist's now. He's a nice young man from Poland; his wife has just had their second child. We have some difficulty understanding him, because it's not long since he left Poland, and his accent is very strong. Needless to say, he can't understand us, either, because he wasn't taught

English with a Welsh accent. His nurse is used to him now, and she interprets if we get stuck, so we get there in the end!

Oh, I've remembered two more things. You'll never guess – someone is going to start a water-bottling business near the spinney, on the right hand side before you go up the hill. I thought Sally was kidding me at first; whatever next!

Padley's twelve acres is going to be converted into a solar farm; I'm sure you'll be able to see part of it from the top road. I feel sorry for anyone who has to look at that every day.

I'll give you a ring in a couple of weeks; take care, and give my love to Dai.

Love from Kath.

xx

Eva opened Barbara's card next, there was note inside:

Killorglin
Hawsker
Christchurch
N.Z.

johnba@mca.nz

15th, August 2006

Hi Eva,

How's things? I still miss you and often think back to your second visit just after Dai retired. Didn't we have a good time during those six weeks?

First of all, Happy Anniversary – fifty-one years!!! Such an exciting time wasn't it, both of us getting married in the same month and me moving out here? Where has all that time gone?

You'll notice that I've included our new email address; it'll be so much easier and quicker than writing letters.

There's going to be some changes at the mill, because a lot of visitors come to this area now; someone we know has asked if they can rent part of our premises and open a franchise. They want to run a small daytime restaurant in the mill; we thought about it, and decided it might be an idea to turn the mill into a working museum at the same time.

Imagine – you enter the mill and the first thing you'll see is the machinery, in roughly in the same place as it is now. Beyond all that, towards the back of the building, is where the restaurant and a gift shop will be; anything we make in the future will be sold only in the shop. I'm quite happy with that, because it's almost impossible to replace the workers as they leave, and I can see that, before long, the machines will cease to operate. The restaurant should be lively, and I see the gift shop selling paintings and crafts made by local people alongside our woven things. It's a pity, but time moves on. Who would have thought sixty years ago that Gorse Wen Farm would become such a successful equestrian and holiday centre? I wonder what your dad would make of it.

Love to Dai, take care, love,
Barbara xx

Eva read Barbara's message again, and immediately went to the computer to send her first email to New Zealand:

Hello Barbara,

Your letter arrived this morning. Thank you, I couldn't wait to try the email. I hope your plans for your mill are successful. The one in Manddiogel does a similar thing; although it only sells beverages and cakes, they get plenty of visitors in the summer months, and the shop is very popular.

I'm okay now, but I want you to know that I've been suffering with depression. It's been building up since I retired. I've tried to shake it off, but, in the end, my doctor sent me to a counsellor. She has been very understanding, and has helped me get things into perspective, she's managed to unravel the jumble that was going around in my head.

As soon as I told her I was Jewish, and had been an evacuee before the war, she understood. She suggested that I suddenly had too much time to dwell on things when I first retired, and perhaps I feel I don't know who I really am, because I know nothing about my real family's background. Apparently it's very common, especially when a displaced person gets older; she's given me a list of contacts in case I'd like to join a support group. I don't think I'll bother, although it's nice to know it's there if I need it. Don't worry about me, I really am all right; I'll cope much better now I know why I feel the way I do sometimes.

I hope this email reaches you okay; give our love to everyone over there,

Love, Eva xxx

It was going to be a busy Saturday, and she decided to take advantage of Dai being out all day with Ron; by now they should be sitting on a damp river bank hoping to catch a fish. She didn't see the attraction herself. She much preferred to put some nice music on and do something productive. When the oven was clean, and all her kitchen cupboards had been wiped inside and out, she made a start on the dinner. Dai was bringing Ron back with him, because he was going to spend the evening with them. She mused over her two letters and reminisced as she made the pudding. She thought of Ron; he and Dai had been friends for over thirty years and were as thick as thieves, despite the fifteen years difference in age and Dai being Welsh, and Ron, Jamaican. She thought it a pity that he and his wife hadn't got back together. As far as she knew, Connie was still in Tanzania; whether or not she had met anyone else she couldn't say. Ron hadn't met anyone; there had been the occasional date that hadn't come to anything. She sensed that he had always hoped that Connie would come home.

After a successful day cleaning, and an unsuccessful day fishing, they ate a hearty meal together. Afterwards the two men set up a game of cards; Eva was tired, so she excused herself and went to bed. In moments she drifted off to sleep with happy dreams:

"Eva, Eva liebling." Frieda Aarons's soft voice gently roused her young daughter; her lovely face smiled down on her sleeping child. Eva stirred and the phantom image of her mother faded; she tried to capture it, but it was gone. She lay paralysed a few moments before consciousness.

Dreams such as this were becoming more frequent with Eva's passing years; they were always pleasant ones, with Mama, Papa, or Iwan. Strangely, she never dreamed of *Kristallnacht*, although sometimes during the day she had flashes of its violence and unbelievable cruelty. She could still hear Mama's screams, people shouting in the street; the sound of Papa, being beaten by those Nazi thugs as they smashed their way through his shop, and trampled his fruit and vegetables into the broken glass on the floor. Eva and Iwan had been asleep in their beds when their shop was attacked, but the loud banging and crashing had woken them; their mother bundled them into the clothes closet and shut the door, leaving them to cower in the relative safety of darkness.

"Had a bad night, love?" asked Dai the following morning.

"Just one of my dreams," she answered, pulling on her dressing gown; she prepared the breakfast, while Dai passed her a comforting mug of tea.

She checked her inbox; there was another email from Barbara. Yesterday her eldest son Jonathan had become a grandfather for the first time. "Barbara and John's great-grandchild has arrived."

"That's good, boy or girl?" he asked, mindful of next door's cat creeping stealthily towards the bird table.

"A girl; they've named her Lucy." Barbara had so many grandchildren Eva had lost count, and now her first great-grandchild was born. Melancholy pushed its way into her thoughts, threatening to bring on a spell of depression. What must it be like to have known your parents and siblings, and to have had grandparents, aunts and uncles, nieces and nephews, children and grandchildren? Barbara had had every type of family member possible, she smiled ruefully.

Dai picked up the all-too-familiar signs and thought this might be a good time to discuss his recent idea with her. "Would you like to move nearer the coast?"

She was taken aback by this bolt out of the blue, "The coast? Which coast?"

"I don't know, the East I suppose, that's the nearest. I'd like to live nearer the sea. After all these years, I still miss having a beach to walk on within an hour from home."

"I'd have thought you'd want to go back to Wales if you want to be near the coast."

"No, we've lived here for well over forty years. If we moved back to Wales, we'd have to start all over again; if we moved to the Norfolk coast, we could still see our friends regularly. It doesn't have to be forever; we can move back if we need to."

She didn't dismiss the idea—in fact she was warming to it; life had got a bit mundane since they had retired. Somehow, without being aware, they had slipped into a repetitive routine. Maybe a house move would be stimulating, and something to look forward to.

"Do you know, I quite like the idea; let's look into it," she said, feeling motivated.

They did look into it, and, after several trips along the North Norfolk coast, they focussed on the villages in Cromer's hinterland. They put their bungalow on the market, and, within three months, had a confirmed offer, and were in a position to start house hunting.

It didn't take long to find what they were looking for, because they had a good budget and there was a lot to choose from. In the end, they chose The Granary, a small and very pretty barn conversion. It had two bedrooms and a tiny courtyard, with just enough room for some planters, a bistro table and two chairs. It was close to a hamlet three miles inland from Cromer. Originally, it had been a grain store annexed to the dairy on a livestock farm. In the 1980s the farm buildings had been sold and converted into barns; the farmer had kept the land, and had rented it to a couple of neighbouring farms.

Chapter Twenty-One
2016

There were no more visits to Wales, because it was too far for Dai to drive these days, although they were able to go back to Leicester from time to time, for a catch-up with old friends. Ron kept in touch, and was a regular weekend visitor. During a recent visit, he and Dai had decided to spend the morning at the recently opened trout lake nearby; fishing from damp river banks was not for Dai any more, but the lake was perfect because the wooden stages, built at intervals around the perimeter, made sitting for any length of time much more comfortable.

During the morning, they chatted about nothing in particular, until Ron mentioned that he was researching his family background. "It's something I've been wanting to do for a long time; I don't know where my family originated—but I guess it was somewhere in West Africa, where one of my ancestors was captured and taken to Jamaica. My surname, Hamilton, is derived from the ancient name of Hameldune; there was once a village called Hameldune, later Hamilton, on the outskirts of Leicester; it no longer exists. I assume that my ancestor was a slave owned by a Hamilton, who had historic links with the village."

"What a coincidence that you are living in Leicester," remarked Dai.

"It is a bit weird, because the rest of my family live in the West Midlands. My mother's parents inherited a three acre small holding in Jamaica, which my sisters and I still own; I think a family member must have been allowed to purchase it decades previously, after the sugar and slavery trade collapsed. My father's parents owned a shop in the Spanish Town area of Kingston and lived quite comfortably, certainly better than the majority of British people at that time. Both my parents had a good education. My mother taught at a school in Kingston and my father was a fireman; during the war he served overseas with the British Army.

"When Britain needed more labour after the war, billboards advertising jobs and a better life in the United Kingdom were erected around the towns and cities of the Commonwealth; my parents were tempted and they emigrated to Birmingham in 1955. Shortly after our arrival, they realised their mistake. The climate was extremely unpleasant compared to what they were used to; they lived in a gloomy back street, and were homesick. My mother worked in a hospital kitchen, my father worked for British Rail as a porter, and we three children had a mediocre education in a run-down Victorian school. When Mum wasn't working, she supplemented our education by teaching us herself; thanks to her, we were able to find good jobs. One sister had a career in education, the other in health care, and I completed my engineering apprenticeship. Connie and I married in Birmingham when we were twenty-two, and, three years later, we moved to Leicester. In the mid-eighties my parents retired and moved back to Jamaica; it was the aim of many immigrants to go home when they retired. My sisters and I were upset about it at first, but their urge to go home was too strong."

Speaking with Dai about his family sparked another train of thought in Ron. "When Eva saw the counsellor a few years back, didn't she suggest that part of the problem might be because she didn't know who she really was, or anything about her family background?"

"Yes that's right; she gave her a list of contacts in case she wanted to join a group of people with similar issues, but she didn't bother."

Ron hesitated a moment, "What do you say about my having a try at finding a cousin? There must be someone out there, surely? I think it would be interesting to find out, and I'd enjoy the challenge."

"What a great idea, but where on Earth would you start with something like that?" asked Dai.

"With you, of course; you know her parents' names and the camp where they died, don't you?"

"Yes, and we have limited knowledge about her brother Iwan too."

"Good. Let me have all the information you have for all three of them: birth dates, where they lived in Germany and where they were captured, send me everything, no matter how trivial."

"Are we telling Eva what we're doing?"

"I wouldn't at the moment; let's see what I find out first. It would be a pity to raise her hopes and disappoint her if I draw a blank. Also, we don't know what's going to emerge from the camps; we might need to be a bit selective with what we tell her."

In the afternoon they had a quick look on the internet at the Belzec extermination camp where Ike and Frieda Aarons had perished. Ron forwarded the information to his computer at home, along with links to the Jewish Virtual Library and other sites that might prove useful.

***

Ten weeks later, Ron had gathered all the information he could find; it was not enough to make a family tree, but he had found someone. He emailed the good news:

Dai, I've searched all I can and I've found a cousin on the maternal side of Eva's family. Her name is Alica Mikuska, she's seventy-four years of age, and she lives in Bratislava, Slovakia. I've included the names of her immediate family, and I think I've got her current postal address which I've included.

I found no additional information about what happened at the camps, so you should go ahead and tell Eva she has cousins in Central Europe.

Such good news,
Ron.

Dai could not wait to tell Eva, and went to find her straight away. To say she was shocked was an understatement. *Who is this person? Has she got the answers to the countless questions that haunt me?* There was not a moment to lose, she began to write to the cousin at the address included in Ron's message.

***

Alica Mikuska took a bank statement and a United Kingdom Airmail envelope from her post box in the foyer, and waited for the lift in the smart block of apartments where she lived; when it arrived, she stepped inside and pressed the fourth floor's button.

Once in her apartment, she made her way to the kitchen and made some fresh coffee. She sat by the window in the lounge, and glanced across the Danube to the castle on the other side of the river. While her coffee cooled, she opened the envelope from

England. It contained a typed letter from an Eva Jenkins. On the attached page, she saw her own name and those of her parents and grandparents, her son Daniel, and his daughter Christina.

Her English was adequate enough to decipher that this person was the only surviving member of the family living in Germany before the war. Her mother told her years previously that several of their relations had disappeared during the Holocaust, and were assumed displaced or exterminated. One of her cousins in Prague registered some of the family's names with groups who had been searching for displaced persons; she assumed that her name must have been found on one of those lists by Eva Jenkins. There was more information, but her English wasn't good enough to understand all of it, so she decided to ask her granddaughter when she came to see her on Saturday. Tina had worked in England for six months, on attachment to a leisure company, and was fluent in English.

On Saturday, Tina arrived at her grandmother's apartment; she was hot and tired after the cycle ride along one of the trails for which she was responsible. This was a busy time for her; it seemed that all of Europe's youth had descended upon this beautiful place to enjoy its leisure facilities. She was employed to ensure that the trails were kept well maintained and safe, which meant that she needed to spend a lot of her time either walking or cycling the routes herself.

"Have a shower if you want; lunch is almost ready," said Alica.

When she was showered and refreshed, Tina sat down at the table, and asked, "Have you had a good week Grandma?"

"I have had a very good week, thank you. Eat your meal, while I ask you something."

"Fire away," said Tina, enjoying Grandma's homemade fish pie.

"I wonder if you would translate something for me; I think you will find it interesting." She took the envelope out of a drawer and put it on the table. "You can take it home if you wish."

While Alica put the bread pudding and cream into bowls for each of them, she glanced at the details. "No need. It won't take long; I'll do it while we have our coffee."

Tina explained that Cousin Eva had avoided her parents' and brother's fate because she had been sent to Wales in the United Kingdom, several months before Britain declared war with Germany.

"Are you going to reply to this letter?" Tina asked. "Would you like me to help you with it?"

"Yes please, shall I compose a reply and email it to you?"

Tina nodded. "Write it in Slovak and I'll translate it into English."

"I'll do it tomorrow; you get off now, you've had a long day," said Alica, putting the rest of the bread pudding into a container for Tina to take home.

"'Bye, Grandma, thanks for the lovely dinner," and, with a peck on her grandmother's cheek, she was gone.

The following morning, Alica wrote her reply:

15th June, 2016

Dear Eva,

What a lovely surprise, when your letter arrived. I did know that one of my mother's cousins and her family had disappeared from Dortmund in Germany during the war, and I am delighted to know that you were taken care of in Wales and have had a happy married life in England. My granddaughter, Christina (Tina) is very fond of England. She spent several months in Suffolk on an attachment with her work, and has friends there.

I'll tell you a little about our family and myself. Our family has been displaced several times during the last two centuries. Eventually, they settled in what is now the north of Austria; this is where our great-grandparents lived and where our grandmothers were born. Your information is correct; our grandmothers were sisters. When your grandmother married, she and your grandfather moved to Dortmund in Germany; my grandparents remained in Austria, and their family continued to live there until it was annexed in 1938. When the Holocaust escalated they fled north across the border, to Czechoslovakia.

When the Nazis invaded Czechoslovakia, my family was sent to a ghetto, where they were put to forced labour; my grandmother worked in a factory, and my grandfather was made to enforce Nazi law as a policeman. He was also made to join the orchestra, which spared him. My parents were very young, and because they were of use to the Nazis, they were also put to work.

I was born in a ghetto in 1942; my days were spent in the kindergarten, while my mother worked in the factory. In 1945, the ghetto was liberated, and my parents settled here in Bratislava. They had two more daughters, Hannah, who lives about ten kilometres from here; and Ruth, who lives in a country village about thirty kilometres to the East.

My husband Henrik died several years ago. We were married in 1964, and have one son, Daniel. Henrik's family were Roman Catholic, from a long line of vintners; when he died, Daniel took over the management of the vineyard and winery.

> *I have sorted out some photographs, and I'll email them to you; these first ones are of our grandparents, Tina and me, and there's one of you with your parents and Iwan. I'm sure you'll be pleased to receive them, because we also lost all our photographs. Fortunately, our relations in America had some and sent us copies.*
>
> *I'm so happy you found me, your cousin,*
> *Alica. xx*

Tina opened her grandmother's draft email. When she had finished translating it, she took a closer look at the attached photographs. There were three: one was very old and taken in a studio; the man was standing with his left hand resting on the shoulder of a seated woman. She knew that this couple were her great-great-grandparents. The next one was taken in the early 1930s. It was a group photograph of Eva's parents and their children; mother was holding baby Eva, and Iwan was standing in front of his father. The third was a recent one, of her and Grandma standing in the apartments' gardens, which lead down to the Danube Riverside Walk. She typed the descriptions and approximate dates underneath each photograph, and forwarded the email to Eva.

It arrived within moments. Eva read it and felt an indescribable sensation when she looked at the group photograph; it was identical to the one which Mama put in her little suitcase when she was sent to the United Kingdom—the one that Nancy had framed and placed on top of the chest of drawers in her bedroom. A duplicate had been taken to America by someone. She wondered who that person was. *Did that mean she had cousins in America too?* She saw her grandparents for the first time in the studio photograph; they were formally dressed and looked very stern. The coloured photograph was of Alica and

Tina taken in a garden earlier in the year; in the background she could see the river and the castle that Alica said she could see from her lounge window.

Weeks passed; Eva and Alica sent each other regular emails, photographs were exchanged, and descriptions of their younger lives in Wales and Slovakia were shared.

It was August now, and Tina was starting to think about how she wanted to spend her annual leave; she was never able to take a holiday during July and August, therefore she usually chose September because the students were preparing their return to education. This year she had an exciting idea; she wanted to go to England and visit her friends in Suffolk. Perhaps Grandma would like to travel with her and spend some time with Eva?

At the same time, Dai was thinking about taking Eva away for their wedding anniversary, not too far away because he didn't drive long distances anymore; he mentioned it to Ron during one of their telephone conversations.

"When are you thinking of going?" asked Ron.

"Our anniversary is September 6th, so any time around then."

"Don't book anything yet, Dai, I've an idea." When they finished speaking, Ron checked his booking for the gig in a Suffolk hotel on 3rd September; it was going to be a reunion of an old 1960s group. He had been a fan when he was eighteen, and had all their records, but had never had the opportunity to see them live. They disbanded in the late sixties, and two of the original five members were deceased. The remaining three had recently been in contact with each other, and had arranged a reunion at a small venue for old time's sake. Paul, the drummer, suggested Grafton Hall in Suffolk because it was a small hotel, recently refurbished by a friend who had sound-proofed the former dining room with the intention of using it for functions.

Ron had originally intended to go for a long weekend, to see the band, and to explore that part of Suffolk while he was there. If Dai and Eva went with him he'd like to stay the whole week; they could do their own thing if they chose to. He rang the hotel to check for availability. There were vacancies, so he provisionally extended his booking, and reserved a double room for them.

He rang Dai again. "How do you fancy a week in a converted gentlemen's residence in Suffolk? It's now a small refurbished hotel, I'm going there for a musical evening on 3rd September. If you like the idea, I can come over to you on the Friday and take us all there on Saturday morning; save you driving, wouldn't it?"

"I think that sounds perfect. I know Eva will want to go; it's years since we went to Suffolk. Did you say you'd made a provisional booking?" Ron said he had, and he would ring the hotel to confirm it.

Dai looked on the hotel's web site, printed the details and took them to Eva. "How about a week in this hotel for our wedding anniversary? Ron's going, because a band he likes from the sixties is playing on the Saturday night; he's offered to collect us, and do all the driving."

Eva looked at the brochure. "It looks very nice; I like the thought of Ron taking us, don't you?"

"I do," he replied. "He said that we must feel free to do our own thing; but if we want to join him when he goes to the places of interest, we will be most welcome to go with him."

When Eva sent her next email to Alica, she included the link to Grafton Hall's site so that she could see where they were going to spend their sixty-first wedding anniversary.

Coincidentally, and simply for interest, Alica showed Tina the online brochure, not realising what her granddaughter had in mind. Tina looked at it, and thought it would be a perfect place for them to stay.

She checked for vacancies before she mentioned it; there was a double room and another with two single beds available, she made a provisional booking for the one with two singles and rang Alica. "Grandma, would you like to go to England for a week in September with me?"

"England!" exclaimed Alica, "Oh yes please, where in England?"

"Suffolk, in the same hotel where Eva and Dai are staying for their anniversary; there's a twin room if we want it. What do you think?"

"It sounds perfect! What about the flights?"

"No problem, there's flights from here to Stansted Airport, and the hotel is only about an hour away. I thought it would be nice to catch up with my friend Rose; she doesn't live too far from there."

"How lovely, a trip to England, I get my granddaughter all to myself for a week, and I shall see my lost cousin for the very first time—this is my treat!"

"Oh no, Grandma, it's too much, we'll go halves."

"No, we won't, you are my only grandchild; if you are prepared to take me all the way to England to see my cousin, I insist I pay for it. Anyway, I'd like to see you enjoy the money while I'm still alive."

"Grandma, you're only seventy-four years old—you have years ahead of you!"

"Let's hope so!"

Chapter Twenty-Two

On the morning of Friday 2nd September, Judy Marshall turned her Range Rover off the main road, and drove down the tree-lined drive leading to Grafton Hall; never before had she performed in a venue such as this. The magnificent building was set in substantial acreage, and oozed class and wealth. It was not a stately home by any means, but a mansion modelled on one. There were three gabled windows set in the grey slate roof, and five bedroom windows equally spaced across the first floor; three stone steps led to an enormous oak door under a portico supported by pillars, and two pairs of French doors flanked both sides of the entrance.

She parked her car in one of the spaces at the side of the house, and went inside to the reception desk. After checking in, she glanced across the foyer to the bar; she recognised Steve and Paul, the other remaining members of the Inside Outfit sitting in comfy leather chairs, chatting over a drink.

Steve was single; he had called it a day after three unsuccessful marriages. Paul was married, although he lived alone because his wife was in a care home. When her Alzheimer's had become so bad that he was no longer able to cope, their doctor had persuaded him to let the professionals take care of her.

Judy was divorced; in the early 1970s she had married a member of a successful rock band. He left her and their two children nine years later, for someone else. Nowadays she was content in her own company, with an occasional evening out with friends, and being a member of the church choir. When her grandchildren were born, she had been involved with their upbringing; now that she was no longer needed to babysit or collect them from school, she found she had time on her hands. A friend suggested she join Facebook; she was sceptical at first, but soon got into it when she realised that most of the people she knew were already members.

One day she received a message from someone called Steve, asking if she was the same Judy Marshall who used to sing in a group; she recognised him instantly, and said she was. After much searching they found Paul; several emails and messages later, Paul suggested a one-off reunion gig in Grafton Hall, for old times' sake. His friend Tony Neilson had purchased the property three years previously, in a terrible state of disrepair. After costing a fortune in refurbishment, it was ready for guests. Paul asked Tony if he would like the band to perform there for an evening to celebrate the opening; he said it would be gratis, if the accommodation and meals were provided with a discount. Tony was happy with his offer, and they all agreed on Saturday 3rd September.

Ron arrived at the Granary, on Friday evening; on Saturday morning he drove Dai and Eva to Suffolk. They stopped for lunch on the way, and, by late afternoon, they were resting in their rooms in Grafton Hall.

Eva was meeting Alica and Tina after dinner, and was nervous at the thought of it; she had not seen any member of her own family since 1939.

Ron was looking forward to hearing his favourite group; he would have given anything to have seen them all those years ago, but to hear them tonight in this lovely venue was going to be worth the wait. He couldn't rest; he decided to go outside and explore the grounds. He walked down to the lake and saw a woman feeding the ducks and swans; she smiled as he approached. "Hello, have you come to tell me off?" she asked anxiously. "I don't think I should feed them, but I love water fowl, so I saved some of my breakfast cereals."

Ron smiled at her. "You're not in trouble; I'm exploring the gardens." She offered him the bag, he took a handful of cereals and tossed them to the birds; when the contents were gone she shook the crumbs from the bag and stuffed it in her pocket.

"This is a lovely place, isn't it?" she said. "I've never been before; apparently it's been closed for a long time. I must say they've made a fabulous job of the refurbishments. I like the way they've kept the character of the building and all the special features downstairs, and yet the bedrooms and bathrooms are right up to date. I was shown the kitchen yesterday; you should see it, any top chef would be proud to work in there."

"It is beautiful," agreed Ron. "I'm here for the week; I've come with some old friends. It's their wedding anniversary on Tuesday. Sixty-one years: can you believe that?"

"No, I can't. Imagine spending sixty-one years with the same person! They must be a very special couple."

"They are, they've known each other since they were six; he says he's loved her for seventy-seven years!"

Ron thought she looked as though she was going to make her way back to the house; he plucked up courage to delay her a while longer. "Are you going back now, or have you time to walk around the gardens with me?"

"I have the time; my name is Judy by the way." She smiled up at him, and in that moment he was lost. They strolled along the path surrounding the lake, completely at ease in each other's company; reluctantly they made their way back to the house. "I really must go now Ron, I have to get ready for tonight."

"Are you going to the gig? Shall I see you there?" he asked.

"You'll see me there; perhaps a drink afterwards in the bar?"

"Definitely! I'll see you in the bar after the show," he replied.

***

"I've eaten far too much," said Dai after dinner, patting his stomach and leaning back in his chair. "There's going to be a few extra inches on the waist-line this week!"

"What waist-line? You lost that years ago!" laughed Eva. "Ron, it's almost eight o'clock; don't be late for the performance."

Ron checked his watch, "I'd better make a move; I hope it's not too late when Alica and Tina arrive. Have a nice time, and I'll see you at breakfast."

Music could be heard through the French doors of the converted drawing room as Tina parked her hired car; she had difficulty finding a space because the car park was full. She dropped her grandmother and the suitcases off at the front door, and parked on the verge, alongside the drive.

While they waited to check in, Tina glanced around the foyer, and noticed a sign on the wall pointing to the lounge and bar; she said to Alica, in a low voice, "That's where we'll meet Eva and Dai. Shall we take our things up to our room and have a quick freshen up first?"

Twenty minutes later, they were downstairs again. Alica opened the door to the lounge, and noticed an elderly couple sitting in one of the huge sofas. They looked up from the magazines they were reading, and, with some difficulty, managed to ease themselves from the squashy cushions. Within moments, Eva and Alica were in each other's arms, shedding tears of joy. Eva was overcome, and was helped back to the sofa by Tina. "I can't believe this is happening," she said, dabbing her eyes. "It is so lovely to see you both."

"We have much to talk about," said Alica, with a strong accent, "—and we have many days to spend together."

While the two cousins laughed and cried, Dai asked Tina if they were hungry. "No, we're fine thank you; we had something to eat on the aeroplane. We'd like a drink, though." Taking charge, she ordered a bottle of wine for herself and Alica, a whisky and ginger for Dai, and a tomato juice for Eva.

Ron managed to find a seat, just before the trio were ready to start. He could not believe his eyes. The female singer in the band was none other than Judy—the lady feeding the birds. How had he not realised who she was? Her hair was short and greying to start with; she looked very different from how he remembered her. Back in the sixties, she had been a chick with long blonde hair and a mini skirt. He had admired her then, but now he was enthralled. He watched her constantly for the next hour, and when the performance was over, the audience gave a rapturous round of applause. Everyone in the room enjoyed it, including the musicians themselves.

While Steve and Paul packed away their guitar and keyboard, a few members of the audience went over to speak to them. Ron, suddenly feeling a bit shy, bought a drink and went to sit by himself in a quiet corner of the bar. He saw Judy enter the room with a small crowd around her; shortly afterwards, Steve and Paul joined them and they became immersed in animated conversation.

He watched her: she scanned the room, she scanned it again. This time their eyes met, and her face beamed; she excused herself and joined him. "Hello, I thought you'd stood me up."

"Er, no," he said, awkwardly; he could hardly breathe. "You were with your friends; I didn't want to intrude."

"I've never met those people before. They said they used to like our music and came tonight because they wanted to hear us again."

Ron said, "I am so sorry about earlier, I had no idea who you were until I saw you on the stage; I came purposely to watch the group too."

Oh my goodness, he's in awe of me, she thought. *Me! A divorced grandmother who lives alone, except for two dogs, and goes to bed after the ten o'clock news every night.* "I'm no one; I sang in a group a long time ago, that's all."

Feeling at ease, he offered her a drink which she accepted; as far as they were concerned there was no one else in the room. They talked and laughed together until quite late. When all the guests were gone, Steve and Paul joined them for a few moments, before going up to their rooms.

"Will you join us for breakfast?" she asked Ron, as they left the bar.

"I would like that; what time do you have to get away tomorrow?"

"Any time, it doesn't matter, it's not a long drive home."

Early next morning, Ron went to Eva and Dai's room and told them that he would be out for most of the day, and that he looked forward to meeting Alica and Tina that evening at dinner. He made his way to the dining room, and waited for Steve, Paul, and Judy to arrive for breakfast.

Steve left as soon as he had eaten, because he lived near the New Forest and wanted to get his four hours' drive underway. Paul lived a couple of hours away; he would like to have stayed longer, but felt he ought to visit his wife. This weekend had stirred emotions, and he was unsettled. He wished things could be different because he was lonely; he had hoped to renew his friendship with Judy—nothing more than that, just someone to go out with sometimes, or to be there whenever he felt low.

He knew she used to like him, but in those days he had never been short of a pretty girl hanging on his every word; he had married one of those girls, and now she was in a nursing home, unable to recognise him.

He thought of his current situation: of Steve doing as he pleased, and of kind gentle Judy. Her new friend had feelings for her, that was obvious, and, by the look of things, she felt the same about him. Suddenly, he felt very weary; the euphoria last night and the nostalgia this morning hadn't helped one iota, and he wanted to go home. He said goodbye to Judy and Ron and went to find Tony who said, "Thanks again Paul, it was a very successful evening; will there be another performance some time, do you think?"

"No, we enjoyed it, but it really was a one-off." He glanced at the splendour around him. "I must say you've made a splendid job of this place; what made you go into the hotel business?"

"It was the house that interested me, not the hospitality part; I employ a manager to see to all that. I have a slight link with the building; during the war, my father was based in Suffolk with the RAF. The house was a convalescent home for burned airmen at the time, and my father used to visit his friends who were recovering after their sorties. When I was a child, we used to go to the Lowestoft area for our summer holidays; he always drove by the house for a look. If I remember rightly, it was a children's home then. In the 1980s and 90s, it was a retirement home for the elderly; but new legislation made it unviable for the owner, and he closed it. He tried to sell the property during the economic crash, but there was no interest, and it fell into decay. I bought it three years ago, with the money my father left me when he died. I've done this for him really, and it's an investment for my children."

"What was it originally?"

"It was a gentleman's residence; I understand it was built during the first half of the nineteenth century as a reward for naval services during the Napoleonic Wars."

"You should put a leaflet together for your guests; I'm sure they'd be fascinated by its history."

"That's an idea, I will. Come back for another visit soon; I hope things improve for you before too long."

Chapter Twenty-Three

Judy took Ron to Southwold for the day. It was his first visit, and she had been looking forward to showing him around; he marvelled at its ancient buildings and history, saying that he had never seen anywhere quite like it. It was almost dark by the time they returned to Grafton Hall; they lingered by Judy's car, neither of them wanting to part. "You really should go now, Ron, or you won't have time to get ready for dinner."

"I'm not the slightest bit hungry." He took her in his arms and held her tight; she looked up at him. "See me again," he whispered. She nodded and promised to return tomorrow.

They had already left for Southwold by the time Eva and Dai met the cousins for breakfast that morning; the four chose a table overlooking the rose garden. Tina declined the Full English because she was in a hurry; she was going to meet Rose and some other friends she had made during her secondment.

After breakfast, Dai found a private alcove in the lounge, where Alica told Eva more about their family's history. "There's quite a lot I can tell you, because our grandmothers were close sisters and our mothers wrote to each other regularly – Mama liked to tell me about the happier times."

"Your grandparents moved from Czechoslovakia to Germany in the early 1890s and settled in Dortmund. I don't know why; perhaps your grandfather's family were there. They owned a grocery shop, and had several children: Frieda, your mother, was their only surviving child."

"Frieda married your father after the first war; he was a local boy from a Jewish family. Your brother was born not long after your grandfather died; your parents took over the shop and looked after your grandmother until her death a few years later. Times were extremely hard in Germany, and it was made much worse for the Jewish community, because during the nineteen thirties, Hitler's Nazis were confiscating their businesses. There were brutal attacks on individuals in the streets; homes were broken into, and valuables legally stolen from their owners."

"I think you know this came to a head during the 9th and 10th of November 1938, *Kristallnacht*. The German authorities looked on and did nothing, while Hitler's stormtroopers and some German citizens rampaged throughout Germany, targeting synagogues, Jewish-owned shops and buildings—smashing windows, burning, looting, beating and murdering. Your family were victims, and they lost their business."

"In December, they heard of children being sent to foster homes in Great Britain; they managed to get you a place on the *Kindertransport*. By January, you were on the train to Hoek van Holland and the boat bound for England."

"With the shop confiscated, and everything of value looted, your parents and Iwan became refugees; they left Dortmund for Czechoslovakia during the winter of 1939. They made reasonable progress, pushing their cart loaded with essential household items and clothing, until the borders closed. Your parents were making their way to my mother, she told me she received a letter when they were not far from Dresden, but there was no word from them after that. We found out years later that they had been among the thousands of Jews rounded up and sent to the camps; Iwan was sent into forced labour in construction, and your parents were sent to Belzec."

"Our family is scattered across the globe; every now and then someone emerges. As far as I am aware, you are our only relative in the United Kingdom; most who left earlier went to America, and those who stayed behind were captured. Of course, when the war ended, we searched, and found that many of our relations had perished. Thankfully, the survivors have been coming to light ever since."

They talked throughout the morning, until Dai thought they all needed a break; he suggested a walk in the gardens before lunch. As they strolled, Eva said, "I think I'm quite clear about what happened, although I don't think I shall ever understand how they could have sent me away with the knowledge that we might never meet again. I have heard it said that those on the *Kindertransport*, who later had children of their own, have asked themselves the same question, and concluded that they couldn't do it; they wouldn't have been strong enough, or they would have chosen to face their fate as a family."

"Desperate times," said Alica, "call for desperate measures; no one knows what they would do in such unimaginable circumstances."

Eva braced herself, "I'm grateful I have you; it means so much to me. I would like us to enjoy this week and get to know each other. When you've returned home, we must keep in touch, and you can tell me the family's news."

"You are an important member of the family, Eva; if you and Dai feel you are able to make the journey, you will be most welcome to come and stay with me, for as long as you wish. Let's go inside now and eat. We have a whole week ahead of us—we must not waste a moment."

They all met in the bar before dinner. Tina, having spent the day with friends, was ordering drinks for herself and Alica. Ron showered, dressed hastily, and went to Eva and Dai's room, "What are you up to, Ron? I've never seen you in such a fluster," asked Dai, knowingly.

"I've met someone; she is the most beautiful person, and she's coming back tomorrow just to see me."

"I can't wait to meet her; be sure to introduce us, won't you?" said Eva. "Let's go downstairs now; I want you to meet my family."

A happy and relaxed evening was spent together. Ron was intrigued by Slovakia, its history and the split with the Czech Republic in 1993; he told them about his family in Jamaica and his life in Leicester. Dai and Eva talked about their early lives in Wales, and their home in England.

The following morning, Judy arrived early; before they left for the day, Ron made sure that she met Dai and Eva. "Join us for dinner; my cousins from Slovakia are here, and I know they would love to meet you," Eva said.

"I will; thank you," replied Judy.

Tina took the three seniors for a drive around the area, "Such pretty villages you have here," remarked Alica. She was enjoying every moment of this English holiday; spending it with her grand-daughter and her new found cousin made it extra special.

There were six for dinner that evening. Judy spoke about her life as a child in Lincoln, and what it was like to be in a pop group during the 1960s; she told them about her home in Cambridgeshire, shared with two Springer Spaniels. "They are lovely dogs, but they do need a lot of exercise; they keep me very active!"

Dai and Eva were taken somewhere every day by Tina and Alica, including coffee and cake at the Nature Reserve nearby, and lunch in the pub in Southwold which Ron had recommended.

Each day before dinner they had a short nap, while Alica and Tina read their books, or spent an hour in the Spa.

Ron met Judy about halfway between her home and the hotel each day; she always brought her dogs, and they explored the local footpaths and bridleways together. On Thursday, Judy had a prior engagement and was unable to see Ron during the day; she joined them all for dinner instead. She was present at breakfast the following morning, and appeared coy when the others arrived looking surprised to see her, "I had a drink last night; I thought it best not to drive home," she explained, blushing.

"And the dogs?" enquired Dai, with a glint in his eye.

"They're at my son's house," she laughed. Everyone else did, too, when they realised her scheme.

On Saturday morning, Alica and Tina left, with promises to keep in touch; Tina drove away, with her grandmother in tears. Reluctantly, the other three returned to their rooms, collected their suitcases, and checked out.

They were all very quiet on the way home, deep in their own thoughts. Eventually Ron spoke, "What would stop you going to see them?" He thought he knew the answer, but asked the question anyway.

Dai replied, "Our age; we're fit enough, but it's risky. It's not like going on a package holiday, with support if something goes wrong."

"What if I were to travel with you, take you to Alica's and stay in a hotel nearby? Would you go then? Bratislava fascinates me, and I would love to see it."

At first it sounded a bit daunting to both Dai and Eva, but their desire to go was strong. "I think we would like to seriously think about it," replied Dai. Eva agreed, she would like more than anything to meet more relations, and see where she might have lived if fate had played a different hand.

"See how you feel in the new year; if you like the idea we can go next May, or perhaps early June," suggested Ron.

"We would love that, wouldn't we Dai?" It was agreed that, if things went to plan, they would go to Slovakia next spring with Ron, and if things worked out the way they hoped, Judy would be going with them.

When they were getting ready for bed that night, Dai said, "Quite a week wasn't it?"

"I can't take it all in," replied Eva.

"Are you coming to bed now?"

"In a while, I'll not sleep yet; I'll sit here for a few minutes and settle my thoughts. You go; I won't be long."

She curled up on the settee, and her mind wandered.

She was a child again, in Wales, with those wonderful people who gave her sanctuary in their home at Gorse Wen Farm; she remembered roaming the hills and valleys with Dai and Rusty, and the chickens she and Stan chose for her birthday at the livestock market, and singing "Ten Green Bottles" in the truck.

She was with Stan in the meadow now: he was showing her how to make a daisy-chain necklace; he held a buttercup under her chin and told her she liked butter. He made funny music from plantains and course grasses, and passed on countless ancient remedies for curing ailments or soothing a sting. He predicted the weather. "Read nature's messages around you," he said. "What are the flowers and insects telling?"

She thought of the love Nancy gave her, and of Glynn and Tom, her surrogate brothers; Tom's wife Kath, her 'mother hen' kindness always ready to share someone's burden. Miss Hughes, cruelly robbed of her fiancé during the first war, who had influenced so many young lives during the dark days of the Great Depression and World War II. And Mary, their angel taken too soon, who sorted everyone out and put them on the right track. So many special people, resting peacefully in that beautiful, verdant haven.

She sighed and her thoughts drifted to Barbara, her dear friend far away in New Zealand, cared for now by her family on the ranch she had left home for, and her little mill with its waterwheel turning slowly in the stream.